CW01653876

Obey the law of the land.

For you

Before a revolution there is realization and revelations', people become weary, tired of the lies, deceit and manipulation. One group of men and women claim to have power over another group of men and women. They plot and scheme behind closed doors. They deceive with words, both written and spoken. Greed is the driving force behind the current mess we are in. Greed, the intense and selfish desire for something, especially wealth and power, has corrupted everything from our birth through to our death. What should be and could be a fantastic experience has been corrupted by the greed of a small number of people, Intent on enriching their time here at the expense of other souls. Most of us have had enough and instead of being told who the enemy is, we have figured it out for ourselves, and we are doing something about it.

It has become necessary to write an account of some recent events, not only to record the happenings, but also to educate people, in readiness for the moment when they finally say enough is enough.

Things have gotten progressively worse. After the first plandemic in 2020 the manipulation of the people continued aggressively. The first pandemic required a multimillion-pound advertising campaign to make it real. The subsequent variants of the virus that were released got weaker and weaker, but the restrictions and removal of our rights continued. Sometimes *they let up a bit, dropping some rules only to bring them back tenfold with the emergence of the flu season.*

The people getting jabbed are spreading the viruses. The restrictions placed on the unvaccinated are almost intolerable. We are viewed as second class citizens, not just by the authorities but by friends and family due to the constant bombardment of propaganda. Our movements are constantly monitored with phone tracking, this is to promote the carbon footprint zones. The excuses for stopping and fining innocent people are being increased by the day. The policy enforcement officers use not only the vaccine cards as an excuse to stop you but now your phone tracking details can be checked, this opens you up for business. Any and all electronic communication is monitored. The main social media platforms are censored and anyone posting the truth is blocked and their accounts deleted. Communication by phone is foolish as everything is recorded. There are curfews in place for most of us and more restrictions are being imposed every day. People are being prevented from working and healthy people are viewed with suspicion.

The farmers have been scared into producing less food and the floods caused by the weather manipulation have seriously harmed the food production still further. Food shortage is the next crisis they are creating, along with the threat of war in Europe. Power cuts, which haven't happened since the seventies, are now commonplace, not because of breakdowns or staff shortages but because of the restrictions, fear and discomfort that they create. A scared population is easier to control.

I have decided to write this account of what is happening in the hope that it will be used to educate future generations and bring the perpetrators of this holocaust to justice. The vaccinated are dying, and despite efforts by the media to distract people from the truth, and the constant censorship of the facts, the reality is that once healthy people are now becoming ill, and company policy is to harass anybody without vaccine status. If you survive the vaccine, then you are charged for your carbon footprint. Some of us are fighting back, good people are having to be violent to protect their friends and family, but we are trying to fight back, not with violence but with knowledge.

1

"Knowledge makes a man unfit to be a slave"- Frederick Douglas

It's a Sunday afternoon and the weather is unusually chilly due to the skies being sprayed to help push the climate change agenda. The unmarked planes have been out all morning spraying their filth into the sky to dim the sunlight. The electromagnetic pulses have been sent up and the signature lines in the sky are visible in the manmade clouds. No doubt it will rain heavily by tomorrow morning.

I am in my garden, a small strip of land at the rear of my modest terraced house, its slabbed over and a small wall runs up both sides, an old wooden shed and a greenhouse takes up half the garden, but the back end has room for a couple of comfy outdoor chairs. The flowers are in full bloom and the fruit bushes are covered in various berries, which provides a tasty treat when I'm watering the garden. The bees are busy collecting pollen, and the spiders are sitting patiently in their webs.

The garden seat is slowly rocking, and a slight metallic squeak is coming from the mounting springs that attach the seat to the frame. My eyes are closed, back straight and I am meditating but as usual my head suddenly jerks upwards, and I was nodding off again. There is not much else to do as an unvaccinated man, we are no longer allowed into the bars, restaurants, cinemas, clubs or even the leisure centers. We are allowed to work and take one hour of exercise each day. The one place they dare not stop us going is church and we take full advantage of this.

Whatever faith you follow you can walk into a spiritualist church and receive a warm welcome. Any color, any race, any belief system and you will be received as the spirit you truly are. This is where I will be heading later to meet some like- minded people to communicate, swap information and get messages.

I drag myself from the comfort of the garden chair and make my way inside to take a shower and freshen up before this evening's service begins. The warm water runs over my body, and I slowly get clean before exiting the shower, drying myself and then dressing. I shout "bye" to my lad, who is busy on his computer, as I'm heading downstairs to put my shoes on. I pull the front door shut as I leave the house and turn left at the end of the short path onto the pavement. The church is only a short walk from my house and as I round the corner it comes into view.

The church itself was built in the late 1800s as a place of peace and sanctuary for the more spiritual in the local community, a rather nondescript and unimpressive building from outside looking more like a single-story workshop rather than a place of worship. An anti-climb fence now surrounds the tarmac car park, and a set of heavy steel gates secures the site from the road but hidden away up a little cul de sac it's the perfect meeting place.

As I get nearer to the church, I see people filtering in through the heavy wooden doors. I glance around as I am walking, looking for any signs of the authorities, but it looks all clear for now. I walk the last few meters up to the door and take a final look around before entering.

I am greeted by the friendly face of Eric, an elderly gentleman who is a regular at the church and he hands me a hymn book. I say "Evening" as I take the glossy binder that contains all sorts of song lyrics and head for a seat. I glance around the church, taking in my surroundings and looking for any unusual faces.

The inside of the church isn't as grand as most churches. There is row after row of chairs instead of pews and a stage with an old wooden rostrum instead of a more ornate pulpit, there`s no stained- glass windows, but obscured glass in the modern plastic frames. The walls have stone plaques built into them commemorating the various dignitary`s and benefactors who have graced the walls and chairs of this sacred place over the years. The building has a smell all of its own and feels very welcoming.

I glance at the large clock on the wall above the stage, it reads 7.29 pm, I hear the clang of the heavy metal gate`s shutting to keep the kids out and the cars safe. Eric the elderly gent pulls the two wooden doors too and turns the key in the old- fashioned lock. The lights are dimmed, and the church secretary makes her way onto the stage where she welcomes everyone and directs us to the first hymn of the night. She fumbles with the buttons on a CD player, and it springs to life. The tune is easily recognizable as ABBA`s I have a dream; this makes me smile as it's not your average religious hymn. We sing with great gusto, and I am smiling as the words come out of my mouth.

After two songs the CD player is turned off and the secretary introduces the medium for tonight`s service. A rather stout lady in her late fifties steps up to the rostrum and looks around the room, she starts to give messages to the many grieving soles in the congregation, but that isn`t why I am here tonight, it`s not a message from spirit that I am after.

Directly to my right but about eight chairs away is my friend Mark. Mark is about six feet tall and physically very fit, although you wouldn`t tell from his outward appearance. Wearing baggy jeans and a loose top, with thinning hair and arms covered in tattoo`s. Me and mark have trained together for many years in various martial arts, we only differ slightly in our preference`s, I am a traditionalist and Mark prefers the modern mixed martial arts, but we happily train together when circumstances allow it, often knocking chunks out of each other in the process. This of course has been limited in the past few years with the movement restrictions, but where there's a will there's a way, and hundreds of hours on the punch bag keeps us sharp.

A discrete glance to my right and I can see a small gold ring on the little finger of Marks left hand, this is a clear sign that he needs to talk to me. This of course can`t be done in the open in case of grasses, or over the phone as all electronic communication is being monitored and it's getting harder to meet face to face with the curfew`s for the climate agenda, so a discrete conversation after the service will have to do.

The medium wraps up her messages for the night and the secretary takes the rostrum again. We join her in reciting the Lord's prayer and she finishes with some announcements of upcoming open days and autumn fairs. The main lights are turned on and we can see each other clearly again. We had lost the light about half an hour ago outside and the brightness of the strip lights made me squint for a few seconds.

"How you doing, kidda" Mark says as he extends his right hand out in my direction. I shook him firmly by the hand and I felt the piece of paper Mark had hidden in his palm slip into my hand. As our hands separate, I slowly close my fist but resist the temptation to put my hand straight into my pocket, instead I trap the slip of paper with my two smaller fingers and extend my index and ring finger out to look more natural. This is just a small precaution as not all the congregation are sympathetic to our cause. The easily brainwashed and the government shills are everywhere, willing to accept the rewards for turning us in. Simple, overheard conversations can get you interrogated, and the sharing of unapproved information is now considered a crime.

I gesture to mark with my left hand towards the tea trolly, as I do this my right hand slips the paper into my coat pocket.

We both move towards the lady serving tea and biscuits and exchange a few pleasantries with her as we are each served a mug of tea. We retreat to the far corner of the church, and we can finally exchange a few words, hopefully out of earshot of any nosey bastards.

"What have you got for me mate?" I ask Mark with a large smile on my face, to the casual onlooker this seems like we are having a few laughs and not up to anything we shouldn't be.

"Just some info and a few web addresses, remember to disguise the search." Mark replied, "Of course mate." We continued our conversation on a lighter note and at a higher volume so anyone listening could hear our exchange. "How`s the missus mate?" I asked, expecting the usual jovial reply.

"Still moaning, she wants the bedroom decorating, but I can`t be arsed mate, you know the score." Mark smiled as he spoke.

"You better do as you`re told or you'll be in the doghouse again." I replied with a laugh. Mark gave me a light punch on the arm which got an even bigger laugh from me.

We returned our mugs to the tea trolley and said a couple of "goodbyes" as most of the congregation were leaving now and only the ladies who ran the church would remain to tidy up the teacups and lock the building up.

Mark takes the arm of one of the old dears as he is leaving and starts to escort her out onto the car park. I smile and nod in Marks direction gesturing that he has pulled, he smiles back and discretely gives me the middle finger, this puts another smile on my face.

I say a couple more "goodbyes" as I am putting my jacket back on. I can feel the reassuring weight of the rice flails that are in a pocket I have sewn into the lining of my jacket. They are divided by a foam pad to stop any unwanted noise. These are a last resort, I can usually talk, punch, choke or kick my may out most situations but if things get a bit on top or I am outnumbered the flails will even things up a bit.

I exit the church through the heavy wooden doors and say "goodnight" to Eric the old fella who is collecting the returned hymn books. I take a good deep breath as the fresh air hits me and turn slightly left to exit the large metal gates. Its only about one hundred meters to my house from here but the short walk can be fraught with danger, as it's the next road over from the busy high street and heavily patrolled by the policy enforcement officers that are quick to make a few quid by handing out their unlawful fines. A decision by a computer that your carbon footprint is high, and they get £50 richer.

The policy enforcement officers (police) love the new powers they have been given and wield these powers with enthusiasm. Since the summer of 2020 the draconian and unlawful measures being forced onto the men, women and even the children by the fake authorities have gotten out of hand. They no longer fight real crime. Burglaries, car theft, muggings and vandalism have been ignored in favor of handing out fines for victimless rule breaking. There’s a rule for everything you do, and a fine that comes with it. They have no real right to fine you but coupled with the fact that they repealed the laws regarding this and altered others to suit their agenda the money is rolling in for the corporations.

The young recruits, freshly brainwashed at the police training centers, believe they have all sorts of power over us, and some of the older coppers are just downright thugs. The good guys have been leaving the force in droves as they can see what`s happening, but the sadistic bastards have stayed and are enjoying the feeling of importance they get from telling good people they can`t do certain things.

As I exit the metal gates a movement catches my eye, coming from my right and

heading straight for me are two coppers. "Evening sir" the taller of the two policy enforcement officers says in his best authoritarian voice.
"I am not a sir, constable, by calling me sir you are implying I have legal title and that`s not true." I reply sharply. His eyes narrow slightly, and a confused look crosses his face. I look directly into his eyes, and I can see the cogs turning as he processes what I just said. "Sorry sir I don't know what you mean" he replies as he takes a step closer. I stand my ground and stare directly into his eyes. I dropped my right leg back slightly to get a better stance. "By calling me sir you are implying I have legal title constable" I emphasize the word "Constable". I take a breath and continue "I have no legal title I am just a man!" A confused look crosses his face again.

His companion a small fat arsed woman with a badly fitting hat, steps forward and says" Don't be like that mate, let's just get a few details and you can be on your way!"

What she means is, if you are stupid enough to give me a name then I can scam a few quid off you.

She removes her notepad from her the top pocket on her stab vest and in true Dixon of Dock Green style, she touches the tip of the pencil to her tongue then puts it to the paper. “Now can I have your name please?” she says with an arrogant tone in her voice.

“Am I obliged to give you a name?” I reply with a question.

“No, you`re not obliged!” she replies, disheartened by my response.

“Am I being charged with a crime?” again responding with a question.

“No, you`re not being charged with a crime” she replied even more dejected this time.

“Am I free to go constable?” came my final question.

“Yes, your free to go!” She replied with a note of indignation in her voice.

I immediately turned and started to walk away. The male officer starts to protest to his colleague, but she silences him by raising her hand. I don’t even look back; I just walk away at a steady pace.

As I round the corner into my road, I immediately increase my pace and almost break into a run as I am only about forty meters from my house. I risk a quick glance over my shoulder, but they have thought better of following me. My hand digs deep into my coat pocket and my fingers find the outline of the single metal key, I retrieve it and get it ready to unlock the door. I glance back for a second time and when I am sure they have not followed me I dart to my right and across the short blue brick path up to my front door. The key slips easily into the well-worn lock and with just a slight turn the door opens. I step inside and quickly close the door behind me.

I take several deep breaths and a sigh of relief, the adrenaline that prepared my body for fight or flight is slowing down now and my heartbeat is getting back to normal. “That’s another lucky escape” I said to myself as I headed for the kitchen to grab a cup of tea.

I knew the policy enforcement officers were trying to get joinder, but because I really had no business with them or the corporations, they work for I avoided any contract. By giving the legal name, for example MR JONH SMITH or MRS JANE SMITH, I would be committing crown copyright theft. I don't own the name that I was given by my mom and dad, and by filling out the birth certificate they gave ownership of the name and me to the crown. When the fat arsed copper said "let's just get a few details mate" what she was really doing is tricking me into doing business with them. It`s called joinder. But I wasn't open for business tonight.

2

"You can't argue with slaves who don't even acknowledge their shackles."

The kettle crackled into life, and I placed a tea bag into my cup. I head for the bottom of the stairs and shout up to my lad "Do you want a drink mate?"

"Yes please" comes the muffled response from his room.

I know he`s on the bloody computer again. His arse rarely leaves his gaming chair unless he wants food, he`s at school or on the toilet, but as I will need his expertise later, I will let him off.

I retrieved the piece of paper from my coat pocket and unfolded it to reveal a handwritten note, it's a link to a video on the internet and next to it Mark had written a few words telling me to take a look.

It's not safe to just type something into a search engine anymore and none of us have used the main search engines for a long time, but even the other less popular ones are monitored and typing the wrong thing in or searching for the truth can get your door kicked off by the policy officers. We don't take any information from the Corporation of Broadcasting bullshit as being true, as they are the propaganda wing of the government. Most of the news reports are scripted to suit the narrative or to distract you from the truth. The social media platforms have so called fact checkers, who basically alter anything they don't like and block or blacklist your account. Information is the best way to beat these parasites and they know it, that`s why there is so much disinformation being pumped out. As fast as the truth is put up it`s taken down again.

I head upstairs with the cup of tea for my lad, as I step onto the landing, I can already see the faint blue glow of the computer screen seeping around the door of his room, and I hear the familiar tip tap of the computer keys as he battles some imaginary opponent in some game or another. I need his help to beat a very real opponent and as I haven`t got much skill on a computer he`s the man for the job.

As I push the door open, I say, "Alright sunshine" and I get the usual glare from him "I need you to work your magic with this please" I continued as I place the cup of tea down on his desk.

"Wait I am in a game" he snaps back at me. I stand around for five minutes or so whilst he completes some imaginary mission, with a final jump, spin and head shot he drops his electronic opponent and then presses a few keys. He presses a button on his microphone and says, "I have got to go off now lads", not waiting for a reply before doing a few more klicks to return the computer to the home screen.

"Let your old dad sit down" I say with a smile, already knowing the response.

"No chance, this is my seat." He barks back at me. We both smile as we go through this little routine every time. "What have we got this time dad?" he says as I hand him the piece of paper.

"A video of some sort I think son." He knows better than to ask where it`s come from as its safer for all the people involved and at 15 years old, he can still get away with saying "My dad told me to do it." I don't know what he does but with several taps of the computer keys he has set up a fake account and made it untraceable. I am fully aware of the risks, as just watching the truth isn`t allowed anymore.

The screen flickers into life and the video starts playing. It`s mobile phone footage and it shows a march of some sorts. I can tell by the flags and comments underneath that it`s from Australia. The footage isn`t very clear and the camera is all shaky but it`s still watchable. It shows the men and women of Australia walking peacefully through the streets of Sydney, they are protesting about the government climate lockdowns, when suddenly the police launch an attack from the left and right at a crossroads. There are screams and shouts of pain from the protestors as batten strikes are landed and a hail of rubber bullets is fired into the crowd, some of the men start to fight back and what was a peaceful protest is now a mass brawl.

A smile spreads across my face as the video plays out on the screen. The protestors are defending themselves and for every copper with a batten there seems to be three or four protesters, they are pouring in from the streets on the left and right. There are several protesters per policy enforcement officer, and they seem to be making citizens arrests. They are using belts, zip ties and even the coppers own handcuffs to restrict the movements of the now not so brave officers. One copper can be heard squealing “We are only following orders.” A protester can be clearly heard saying “I am arresting you for assault and attempted murder!” The policy enforcement officer’s helmet is removed, and he is clearly bewildered.

The video ended with the camera turned in the direction of the young man who was filming, he raised his fist in the air and say`s “Welcome to the revolution!”.

I was still smiling as the screen went blank and the video went off. My lad pressed a few buttons on the keyboard and his game popped back up on the screen. I ruffled his hair before leaving the room and I got the usual dig in the ribs.

I made my way downstairs and headed for the lounge, I plugged the TV in to the wall socket and fumbled with the remote control. We don't leave electronic devices plugged in, this isn't for environmental reasons but for privacy, the devices are always watching and always listening, but they need power to do this. The TV flickered into life, and I typed the number for the Corporation of Broadcasting bullshit. The ten pm news was just starting, the titles finished playing and the news reader started reading the pre scripted disinformation. A report about vaccine saving lives and how brave the nurses are for working through the latest pandemic, in the very next breath he tells us how the ministers have voted to cap health workers pay rise at 1.5%, and to force any unvaccinated health workers out of their jobs. Next came more drivel from some so-called expert telling us that the climate change deniers are a danger to the country and if we would only give them more money, they would make the climate problem go away. The screen cut away to the next report and it was the exact scenes I had just watched upstairs.

The news reader spoke over the video "And in other news, Australia`s brave police officers were confronted with an angry mob of climate deniers today in disturbing scenes from Sydney. Officers wearing riot gear and using rubber bullets were attacked by an angry mob, a spokesman for the police said." "Sixty police officers were attacked by a group of over one hundred protestors, but police used reasonable force to stop the troublemakers."

The video only ran for about fifteen seconds and only showed the protestors fighting back, the police attacking the protestors and the protestors disarming and making citizens arrests on the police officers was conveniently not shown as usual. I pressed the red button on the TV remote and the screen went blank. I removed the plug from the wall socket and checked the pieces of black tape were still over the camera and microphone holes on the tv.

I headed back upstairs and along the landing into my lad's room,

"I have already done it before you ask" he said curtly.

I raised my fist and shook it in his direction, he just smiled at me. He knew the score and he had created a fake profile on all the social media platforms. Every time we get a new video or piece of information, he uploads everything again only for it to get taken down within a couple of days but in those two days hundreds of thousands of people get the information they need to see. The so-called fact checkers are nothing, but paid shills and they censor anything the government doesn't like.

My lad shuts the computer down and heads along the landing and into the bathroom to get a shower before bed. I go back downstairs into the lounge and retrieve the mobile phone from the drawer where it's kept in a metal tin. The metal tin acts as a faraday cage and prevents the phone from transmitting or receiving. I only use the phone, when necessary, mainly for work. We don't carry phones with us when we are out and about and up to "special work" as the ladies at the church call it.

The phones are constantly tracked, and the microphones and cameras can be activated by the powers that be at any time, we never have conversations near a phone, computer or TV because we know they are watching and always listening, they can pinpoint our position too within 3 meters and they can tell if two or more people have met up just from this information.

I press the button on the side of the phone and the screen lights up, and after a few seconds I can check my calls, texts and emails. Nothing to report which is good, we don't do anything that leaves a digital footprint.

3

"Things are not getting worse they are getting uncovered. We must hold each other tight and continue to pull back the veil." Adrienne Maree Brown.

After a long day at work, I headed for the supermarket, only to find they have restricted shopping for the unvaccinated to a Wednesday only, so I didn't argue, I just headed for a local shop and stocked up on some essentials. Of course, the government is spouting more shit to justify these measures, saying if we would all just comply and be obedient little sheep then everyone would benefit. We know its bullshit, the only people benefitting are the friends and family of the MP's. they are giving VIP contracts out, for anything from a face mask to a syringe, one parasite MP even opened a company in his wife's maiden name and awarded her the contract to supply plastic disposable aprons at ten times the real value of the product, but that's how the scam works, it`s a big club and we as the public aren't in it.

I pulled up in the work van and reversed into a space on the road, about five doors down from my house. I retrieve the shopping bags and head for my front door, as I turn onto the blue brick path I glance down and see the half end brick that is kept behind the wall has been moved, I know who has moved it and it's a sign that someone needs to speak to me. The meeting will be later that evening at a pre-arranged place and time.

I put the key into the lock on the front door and with a slight turn the lock clicks and the door opens, I push the door and step in with the shopping bags, I am home but not for long tonight. I make my way through the house and into the kitchen, I open the fridge and carefully pack the food away and turn the oven on to warm up before heading upstairs for a shower. I stand in the shower for a good fifteen minutes, washing the grime and dust from work off me. I exit the shower and dry myself and put on a fresh set of clothes.

I head back downstairs and put two frozen pizzas in the oven as there's no time to demonstrate my legendary cooking skills tonight, which I'm sure my lad will be glad of. I busy myself with a bit of cleaning and tidying up whilst tea cooks.

"Tea`s up son." I shouted from the bottom of the stairs, and I immediately heard the thud of his footsteps along the landing.

Me and the lad sit and chat whilst eating our tea together. After ten minutes clearing the tea stuff away and washing up I put my boots on and lace them up , I retrieve my coat from the hall way and check the pockets to make sure I have nothing that can identify me as a legal fiction , I check the rice flails are still hidden in their little pocket and the foam packer is still in place to prevent any unwanted noise , I put the coat on and jump up and down a couple of times , I am confident there's no noise from the flails.

I shout up to my lad "Bye son, love you. Remember the plan"

He knows the plan off by heart, if for any reason I don't come home he waits until the next morning and leaves for school as normal but calls into my sisters on the way and lets her know I didn't come home, she in turn lets my brother-in-law know and he puts the feelers out to find me. It hasn`t come to that yet and I hope it never does but it's best to be prepared.

I leave the house locking the front door behind me. As I walk along, I gently push my left arm against my side, this pushes the rice flails into my body and gives me a bit of reassurance.

The walk to the park is about fifteen minutes, and as most people do their exercise hour after tea, it's busy. It`s a pleasant evening and there's the smell of autumn starting to come through. Moms and dads are juggling an array of scooters, prams, bikes and kids, whilst heading for the park to run around and burn off as much energy as they can in an hour. There's a steady flow of traffic on the main road and a moped is stopped at the traffic lights, the petrol and two stroke oil fumes from its exhaust are hanging in the air. The lights change and the moped squeals as it pulls away and disappears down the road in front of me, long before the noise fades out.

I finally reached the entrance to the park and two young ladies were jogging towards the gate, I stopped and gestured for them to come through and the one at the front smiled at me. I gave her a wink and walked through the gate, glancing back at her as I did.

The avenue that leads down to the park has the old park keeper's cottage on the left. It's a Jacobean style lodge but according to the date stone it was built in 1908. The windows are boarded up and It's never been occupied in all the years I have been coming here. There's a car park entrance off to the right and a row of blossom trees lining either side of the road. In spring the trees burst into life with pink and white blossom, and the avenue is awash with color for a few weeks, but as its august the trees are in leaf, and there's no sign of the autumn colors yet. At the end of the avenue the park opens out, with a kiddies play area off to the right and a skate park with the usual gathering of teenagers practicing smoking, swearing and the odd bit of scooting.

I know exactly where I am going and who will be there, but as usual I will walk a longer way around and make the meeting look more casual rather than planned. Walking straight across the football pitches and up to someone would be a dead giveaway, plus if the coppers have the drones flying about and spying on people then we will walk straight past each other without stopping.

As I am walking around the park, I see the familiar blue jacket of the mate I am meeting, I also see his rather large and intelligent Alsatian dog, who upon seeing me raises his ears and charges in my direction to greet me, stopping just short of me and springing in my direction landing with both front paws on my shoulders, nearly knocking me over. Hardly a discreet meeting but my mate has the dog well trained and calls him off as he`s walking up to me apologizing profusely. To the casual onlooker it would appear the daft dog just jumped up a stranger, nearly knocking him over and the owner running up apologizing. I am now fussing the dog and saying, "Don't worry about it mate" and this gives us the excuse to have a little chat. We don't walk together as we were heading in different directions, but we are safe to talk for a minute or two.

Alan is a heavy-set man in his late fifties, I know he lives near the park and he`s really into the law side of what's going on, it`s Alan who provides the lawful solutions to the problems us people have, these solutions come at a small price, and Alans's price is an ounce of weed as none of the medicine his doctors prescribe can touch his arthritis like cannabis can. I discreetly pass the bag of smelly green stuff over to him and in return he hands me a thick envelope which I immediately tuck inside my jacket. We exchanged a few words of mutual thanks, I fuss Ralf the Alsatian, and Alan, again apologizes for the dog's behavior, just loud enough for a couple of passersby to hear him. We part company in different directions.

This is the risky part now, because if we were being watched and someone saw the exchange taking place then both of us have illegal stuff on us, and ironically, I would get into more trouble for having bits of paper with the truth printed on them than Alan would for the weed.

I continue to make my way around the park, the sun is slowly setting now and although it's approaching dusk, I see the familiar outline of two policy enforcement officers entering the park through the top gate. I can't change direction now as it would raise suspicion and I have no choice but to walk past them. Although I haven't done anything wrong as such, they don't like the sort of information I am carrying. I once again push the rice flails into my body through my clothing with my left arm, a pang of excitement reaches my stomach. The adrenaline is slowly being released and I start to go through my words for if I am stopped.

With the approaching dusk, the bright yellow vests of the officers are aglow and the distance between us decreases with every step. I will try and talk my way out of any confrontation first then resort to the flails if I need them. Twenty meters between us, now ten and five, four, bang out of nowhere and with perfect timing, Ralf the Alsatian runs right into one of the policy enforcement officers, closely followed by a rather breathless Alan who again starts apologizing profusely for his dog. Alan, despite being breathless, is drawing heavily on a cigarette to hide any smell from the weed in his pocket. The officer, who must be a dog lover, is now fussing with Ralf and rubbing behind his ears. I hear the start of a conversation between Alan and the officer "He`s a big lad, how old is he?" and although Alan would have answered I am past the officers and heading out of the gate before I hear the reply. "Thank you, Alan and Ralf, I owe you one" I say quietly as I continue along.

The rest of the journey home was uneventful. I occasionally glanced back over my shoulder to check I didn't have any unwanted company but as far as I could see I was all good, just to be on the safe side I went about ten paces past my house then quickly turned around to catch anyone darting into the shadows, but it was all clear. With a quick turn of the key the lock opened, and the door swung inwards, my nostrils immediately filled with the smell of home, and I breathed a sigh of relief.

Although its only august it`s rather cold in the house, the weather manipulation technology can alter the temperature, making the climate scam seem more real. I place some kindling into the log burner along with a fire lighter and a couple of small logs, with just a touch from the gas lighter the little white paraffin-soaked block ignites, and the flames quickly spread. I shut the burner door and open the air vent; this sends air into the mixture and the fire soon takes hold.

As I am heading for the kitchen, I retrieve the large envelope from my jacket pocket and tuck it under my arm. I open the fridge door and the light illuminates the room as I reach in to grab a beer. I close the fridge and head back to the lounge, which is now warming up nicely, I know I will regret lighting the burner in about half an hour when the room is too warm, so I close the air vents to quell the flames. I slump down into my comfy settee and take a long swig of beer before ripping the top off the envelope. I pull out several pieces of paper, some pieces are links to websites and encrypted links to this and that, but one piece catches my eye, I put the rest of the papers down on the settee next to me as most of its computer codes and links that I will need my lads help with but the one in my hand Is written in good old understandable English, so I begin to read.

There are no manmade laws. There are manmade rules and regulations. The rules and regulations only apply to consenting members of society. Any of us can create a membership club and assign rules to it. That does not give the creators of the club the authority to force their club rules onto nonconsenting men and women who are just going about their lives. The society that the government forces its rules on to, is no more than a membership club. No different to a sports club, bird watching club or gardening club. The rules of the club have no real authority, other than the degree to which they can intimidate, coerce, bully and trick others into obeying them, with their monopoly on force. We have sovereignty, me, you and everyone else, and we always have had it. The illusion of their authority is dissolving. The authorities are making a final attempt to consolidate their self-proclaimed power. We know this and they know it. We are sovereign. Author unknown.

I place the piece of paper down on the settee next to me and edge myself forward, I push myself up with the usual groan of a man my age. I go through the door into the dining room and rummage on my bookshelves for a dictionary, blowing the dust off it as I lift it down.

Returning to the lounge I slump back down onto the settee. I thumb through the dictionary until I get to the letter S, I slow down and turn to the individual pages until I find the word I am looking for.

Sovereign

Noun

1. A supreme ruler, especially a monarch. “The emperor became the first Japanese sovereign to visit Britain.”

Adjective

1. Possessing supreme or ultimate power. “In modern democracies the people`s will is in theory sovereign.”

It often describes a person who has supreme power or authority, such as a King or Queen, Nations and states are also described as “sovereign” this means they have power over themselves, their government is under their own control, rather than under the control of an outside authority.

I flick back through the pages until I reach the letter A, I use my finger to keep the page whilst I reach down and pick my beer up, I take a good long swig from the bottle then return it to the floor. I turn back and forth until I find the word Authority, then I take in the definition.

Authority

Authority is the ability of a person or organization to conduct a certain lifestyle for another person or group. Authority is made by a certain social power. The power might be materialistic (such as a threat to harm someone) or fictitious (such as a belief in a certain person's power).

"Interesting" I say out loud as I close the dictionary. The book makes a loud thump sound as it shuts. I throw the heavy book onto the pillow next to me before reaching down for my beer. I sat quietly, deep in thought for a while. I heave myself up again and take a pen and note pad off the sideboard before sitting down again. I feel I need to write my thoughts down.

The only power these men and women who believe they are in authority have; is the power we give them. I am sovereign; you are sovereign; so, what makes these men and women different from me and you, a few words spoken in front of a judge? An oath of office, who says that matters? It`s* *just a group of men and women who at some time in the past gave themselves the right to give another bunch of men and women some fake authority. It`s only their belief that they have power over someone, and that someone believes that to be true. They have created a whole web of lies to make all this authority seem real. It`s very true that we need policemen and women to arrest criminals, rapists, pedophiles, murderers and fraudsters but when there is no victim there is no crime. What is going on now is a crime against the men, women and children of every country and every nation. The policy enforcement officers, and local councils are giving out thousands of pounds a day in fines for everything from going a few miles over the speed limit to being out after a certain hour of the day, all these fines are unlawful, and we have the right to decline them.

I take another mouthful of beer and let my head tip backwards onto the cushion behind me then I just stare at the last few dying embers of the fire. The danger of thinking too much at this time of night is that I won't sleep and the realization of what is being done to us makes me angry. I snap out of my daydream with a jolt, the fire is completely out now and a quick glance up at the large clock on the wall tells me it's time for bed.

4

"You must never be fearful of what you are doing when it's right."

Rosa Parks

I turned up to work today, only to be told that after a meeting yesterday and because of pressure from the government, the company I subcontract to has decided to adopt the no jab, no job nonsense. I didn't argue, I just unloaded a few of their materials from my van and drove off. I hadn't got a mile down the road and the phone rang; I could see from the caller ID on the screen in the van that it was the boss of the company that had just let me go. I reach across and press the green phone icon on the screen and the speakers come to life.

“Dan, it`s Adam from Pinnacle Construction” says the familiar voice of the contracts manager.
“Hi Adam, how you doing?” I politely enquire. “Not so bad mate, how about you?” he says. “I’ve had better mornings” I say sarcastically. “That’s what I wanted to talk to you about Dan, mate.” Adam replied.

So, suddenly, I’m his mate, ten minutes ago he was throwing his weight about, saying the unvaccinated are a danger to the other members of the team, just before he told us that we had to leave.

“We have had a rethink and if you would be willing to get the vaccine within the next two months, we may be able to keep you on” he says with a hint of desperation in his voice.

“I won’t be getting vaccinated as long as I have a hole up my arse Adam, and as I am sure you are aware I am the only man you had working for you that does what I do; Now I have several other people offering me work, vaccine or no vaccine, so I will be contacting a few other people. I wish you all the best, and if in the future you all come to your senses and stop this vaccine nonsense, then give me a call but for the mean time I will say goodbye."

With that I pressed the red part of the screen, and the phone went dead, the radio came back to life and by chance the song "I'm free" by the soup dragons is playing. I turn up the volume and sing at the top of my voice "I'm free to do what I want any old time." A huge smile crosses my face and I know it will be ok.

Due to my unexpected day off I have time to sit in the garden and delve a bit deeper into some of the information I have been getting. My lad who is still off school for the summer holidays, sets me up with the old iPad we have. It`s a bit dated and must be plugged into the mains via an extension cable up into the garden, but it's usable.

He sets up another fake email and he makes my searches untraceable. I sit rocking slowly back and forth in the comfy garden chair.

The temperatures are not too bad today, and despite the attempts of the media to push the climate change agenda common sense is telling me it's all bullshit. I swipe the screen on the iPad, and it wakes up. I opened the large envelope I picked up off Alan yesterday evening, I thumbed through the pieces of paper and stopped at one that caught my eye. It had suggested searches written at the top of a long-handwritten list. I started to type slowly with one finger "What is a policeman's oath?" the screen slowly loads up and I click on the first answer.

I do solemnly and sincerely declare and affirm that I will well and truly serve the king in the office of constable with fairness, integrity, diligence and impartiality, upholding fundamental human rights and according equal respect to all people; and I will to the best of my power cause the peace to be kept and preserved and prevent all offenses against people and property and that I will to the best of my skill and knowledge discharge all the duties thereof faithfully according to law.

I take a deep breath and stretch my legs out, the afternoon sun is getting warm now and someone has lit a barbeque nearby, the smoke is blowing across the garden. I take a swig of orange juice from the glass that is to my right then read the next search suggestion on the list. I start to type into the search bar again "What is the Kings oath?" I clicked on the first answer again and read a small passage about the coronation. It involves the Archbishop of Canterbury asking the King questions and the King replying, "I will."

Archbishop "Sir, is your majesty willing to take the oath?"

King "I am willing."

Archbishop "Will you solemnly promise and swear to govern the peoples of the United Kingdom of Great Britain and northern island, Canada, Australia, New Zealand, the union of south Africa, Pakistan and Ceylon, and of your possessions and the other territories to any of them belonging or pertaining, according to their respective laws and customs?"

King "I solemnly promise so to do."

Archbishop "Will you to your power cause law and justice, in mercy, to be executed in all your judgements?"

King "I will"

Archbishop "Will you to the upmost of your power maintain the laws of God and the true profession of the gospel? Will you to the upmost of your power maintain in the United Kingdom the protestant reformed religion established by law? Will you maintain and preserve inviolably the settlement of the church of England and the doctrine, worship, discipline and government thereof, as by law established in England? And will you preserve unto the bishops and clergy of England, and the churches committed to their charge all such rights and privileges by law do or shall appertain to them or any of them?

King “I will”

With a couple of swipes and clicks I return the iPad screen back to the search bar. I take another sip of orange juice and a rather large breath of barbeque smoke. A radio bursts into life a few gardens away and my peaceful afternoon is ruined. Despite the noise I managed to go deep into thought. Having read the two oaths it would appear the police take an oath to the King and not to the government, the King swears to uphold gods’ laws which are the common laws of the land not the maritime laws of the sea being forced upon us by the parasitical government.

The music is getting louder and with the number of voices and laughter coming from the garden I can only presume the barbeque smoke is part of the same party. I press back on the screen and wake the iPad up again; I type into the search bar “what is a judge's oath?" The screen slowly loads up and there are several answers, so I click on the top one and start to read. It looks like they take two oaths collectively referred to as the judicial oath.

Oath of allegiance

I, JUDGES NAME, do swear by almighty god that I will be faithful and bear true allegiance to His Majesty King Charles the third, his heirs and successors, according to law.

That's interesting still no mention of politicians, I read on

Judicial oath

I, JUDGES NAME, do swear by almighty god that I will well and truly serve our sovereign King Charles the third in the office of ??????? and I will do right to all manner of people after the laws and usages of this Realm, without fear or favor, affection or ill will.

Again, I scroll back to the search bar screen. I put the iPad down and rested my head back onto the comfy cushion on the swing seat. The party a few doors down is in full swing now and the charcoal smoke is now mixed with various food smells and by the smell of it, it's getting well and truly cremated if I am any judge of cooking. I close my eyes and start to think.

After about five minutes I open my eyes, I quickly pick up the pen and paper I have next to me and start to write my thoughts down again.

It`s all deception, nearly everything the government does involves some sleight of hand, fraud, coercion or just downright criminality. The police take an oath to the King and swear to keep the peace but regularly we see them beating people up who are peacefully protesting. The judges take an oath to the King and promise to uphold the laws of the realm without fear or favor, but time and time again they favor *the outcome with the most money and least embarrassment for their mates.*

I finished writing and put the pen and paper down.

A loud cheer goes up and the song "Happy birthday" is being recited rather loudly from the barbeque party, I finish the remainder of my orange juice and after putting the cushions from the chairs away and wrapping the extension lead up, I head inside to take a shower.

I remove the shower head from the riser rail and turn the shower on, as soon as the water is up to temperature, I place the shower head into the rail and stand directly under the jet of water. My mind is racing now. It seems the deeper I dig looking for the truth the angrier it makes me. I have more questions and I am hoping the iPad has the answers. I wash the last of the soap from my body and eventually turn the knob on the shower to stop the water, I exit the shower and dry myself, still forming questions and making a mental note to dig much deeper.

5

“Until you wake up, we will fight for you.”

I started working for an old friend today, I wasn’t asked for a vaccine card, no interview or any nonsense, he was genuinely happy just having someone he could rely on and I’m sure with just a few days getting used to the new job sheets everything will be ok.

It’s Wednesday evening and as usual I’m off to the spiritualist church. It`s the last day of august and the sun is going down, the red sky being cut through with the streaks of chemicals from the airplanes. I gently push the weight of the rice flails in my coat against my body as I walk. I use my right hand to find the GoPro camera that my lad has lent me, it was his idea to carry it to record unlawful policy enforcement stops that we are constantly subject to. I make a mental note to tell Mark if he`s at church tonight. The GoPro is untraceable unlike the mobile phones and from what my lad said it should film for at least an hour on a full charge, if not more, so any footage of the unlawful stops can be used as evidence against the coppers.

I reach the large metal carpark gates at 7.20pm and head straight through them and up the small ramp and past the large wooden doors. Eric the elderly gent on the door's hands me a hymn book and I say "Evening" as I take the plastic covered booklet from him. I walk down the center isle to the 3rd row of chairs on the left and I take the chair nearest the isle. I glance over to my right but there is no sign of Mark. A few more people enter the hall and I get a glimpse of Mark entering to my right, I glance over without acknowledging him and look at his left hand. There's no ring on his little finger, this means he has nothing for me tonight, I however have the information from Alan in the park, the oaths of office and the GoPro idea to pass on. I have already slipped the small gold ring onto my little finger and Mark will have spotted it straight away upon entering.

The ladies who run the church know exactly what we get up to and they have unofficially called us the Warriors of light. Unfortunately, most of them got vaccinated in the first wave before anyone knew about the side effects, but they are a hardy bunch, and they suffer in silence. They know we are on the side of good and they help us as much as they can without drawing attention to themselves. They have hidden the odd bit of information or ensured the message got through depending on what was needed. Being vaccinated they have free movement on their side whereas us unvaccinated are subject to harassment on a daily basis.

7.28pm and the doors are due to be locked at 7.30pm. There is a commotion outside, me and Mark glance at each other but we know better than to get involved, we stay seated as two policy enforcement officers walk into the church. They are met almost instantly with an army of old dears who are well versed in dealing with these intrusions.

"Yes, officer how can we help you? Are you here for the service?" says Anne, a rather plump and feisty lady in her sixties.

"No madame we are just checking people's vaccination status" says the taller of the two officers.

"Well as you know officer, we welcome everyone here, any race, religion, vaccinated or unvaccinated, even you are welcome but if you're not staying for the service then you need to leave so we can lock the doors" came the smart reply from Anne. The policy enforcement officer was either too stupid to understand Anne`s little dig or he just didn't register it but after a good look around the two officers turned around and exited the church. I heard the heavy metal car park gates shut, closely followed by the heavy wooden doors, and breathed a little sigh of relief.

We settled down and the service began. After a quick rendition of I have a dream by ABBA, which raised the mood in the room considerably, we recited the lord's prayer, then tonight's medium takes the rostrum. Her name is Sarah and from what I have seen of her in the past, she is very gifted. Sarah`s eyes scan the room, and she begins to give messages to various people, bringing comfort to the bereaved and a smile to most the faces in the room. If there are any tears, then those tears are of love. After the fourth message, Sarah spoke directly to me.

"I am with the gentleman in the black top" she says whilst pointing in my direction. "I have a man in spirit with you, he`s about seventy years of age and he`s bald, he is giving me the name James, can you take this man?"

"I can take him thank you" I reply. I already know who's around me, as I'm quite switched on to the spirit world and it`s nice to get a message.

"This man says you have a challenge ahead of you, or something you are aiming for, can you understand this?" Sarah says with confidence.

"I can" I reply again.

"You will be ok with this challenge, and you will get the outcome you want, but there is a period of discomfort coming up, you will come out of the other side a better person. This man sends you his love and he is proud of you; he says you are a chip off the old block."

"Thank you" I reply with a large smile on my face. Sarah moves on to the next person and I continue to listen to her messages.

As the time approaches nine pm, Sarah starts to wind the service down, we say a closing prayer and Anne stands up and does the general announcements and notifications for some open days and an upcoming autumn fair, with a round of applause for Sarah the medium, the service is over. Right on cue one of the old dears appears from the back room with the tea trolly. I don't usually hang around long if I can help it, but I need to pass the information on to Mark, he has been accosted by a lady called Sylvia and once she starts talking, she doesn't stop. I see Mark nodding politely and smiling in all the right places. I take a cup of tea from the trolley and exchange a few pleasantries with the lady who has served me. Mark finally escapes from sylvia`s clutches and slowly makes his way to the door. I quickly finish my tea and return the cup to the trolly lady, a quick "Thank you I'll see you next week" and I too am heading for the door.

The small hallway between the main church room and the heavy wooden doors is about six feet long, I time my exit so that I am directly behind Mark, I hand my hymn book back to Eric the doorman and without pausing thrust the envelope containing the information into Marks hand which he has behind his back ready to receive the discrete gift. We don't even exchange a word.

As we exit the large wooden doors a blast of chilly autumn air hits us, Mark immediately turns right to head for his car, and I go left and walk towards the metal gates at the end of the car park. I hear the beginnings of a conversation between Mark and another church goer, but I am out of earshot after just a few paces and the voices become a blur. I am only about one hundred meters from the safety of my house and a bottle of beer before bed, but experience tells me not to drop my guard.

Out of nowhere one of the two policy enforcement officers who Ann fobbed off earlier appears just slightly ahead of me. A shiver goes through me as the adrenaline fills my body.

"Excuse me sir" the officer said as he blocked my way.

“I am not a sir constable, by calling me sir you are implying that I have legal title and I don’t, I am man, nothing more, nothing less.” Came my well-versed reply.

“Are you trying to be clever with me?” the copper grunted.

“Are you here on your oath tonight constable?” I asked politely. By calling him constable and asking about his oath I am trying to remind him he is here as a peacekeeper and not to force government policy onto me. I quickly took the GoPro camera out of my pocket, I had switched it on as soon as he stepped out of the shadows, I hoped it had caught the conversation so far but as it was in my pocket it may not have.

I pointed the little camera at the officer, and he immediately turned nasty.

“Get that fucking thing out of my face, you’re not allowed to film me working” he snapped aggressively.

"You're a public servant and we are in a public place constable, now charge me with a crime or move out of my way so I can go" I said standing my ground "I am filming for my protection and yours constable" I tried again to make him see sense.

"Give me your details." He snapped again.

"Am I obliged to give you a name?" came my sharp response.

"I don't give a fuck if your obliged or not now give me your details or ill fuck you up." he barked.

"Let's start with your detail's constable, what's your name and number?" my response angered him even more.

"Fuck you" he squealed.

I was in the shit here, this cunt had removed his collar numbers, and he was on his own, it would be my word against his and I know who`s side the corrupt judges would be on.

"Stop resisting" he shouted for the benefit of anyone in earshot. I looked at him a bit confused, but a quick look around revealed there was not a soul in sight.

"Stop resisting and get on the floor" he shouted louder this time. I had to think quick, this cunt was setting me up for resisting arrest and no doubt assaulting a police officer and I hadn't done either.

"Taser, taser, taser" came the next shout as he reached for the grip of the yellow gun in the chest holster, his hand wrapping around the handle and his arm thrusting in my direction. The weapon made a small click as he pulled the trigger. Now in all the training this prick had done, and I should imagine on all the previous occasions he had shot this deadly weapon at some poor soul, the victim falls to the ground and is fucked, well not on this occasion sunshine. As he drew the weapon I had turned to my right, reducing my profile to not much more than an arms width coupled with the fact that my coat is quite thick and the prongs couldn't penetrate the canvas, meaning the taser gun did fuck all to me. I looked him in the eye and said, "Now that's attempted murder." PC plod was desperately fumbling for another weapon. I dropped the GoPro, which was hopefully still recording the attack. I closed the distance between me and the very wide-eyed officer.

Now in Karate we use a technique called uraken gyaku tsuki, it's a back fist followed by a reverse punch, and the thousands of times I have practiced that combination during training really paid off tonight because that's exactly what hit this cunt, a perfect Uraken gyaku tsuki combination. Just as the knuckle of my left hand contacted with his jaw the right seeking knuckle was finding its target too, he was unconscious before he hit the floor. Now you may think that should be it, but this cunt tried to set me up and he could have taken my life with his taser gun and taken me away from my son, so fuck him.

I reached into the left side of my jacket with my right hand and tightened my grip around the handle of the flails I had in my coat. I casually swung the flails up and over my right shoulder, there was no time for any of that fancy Bruce lee shit, flinging them around my body and showing off, no I just simply brought them down onto his skull, once, twice, three times, each time the flail landed it made a sickening thud. Fuck him, if he lived the chances are he would be brain damaged and if he died well that's justice as the cunt could have killed me for refusing to join in his game.

I quickly slipped the flails into my pocket and grabbed the GoPro off the ground. I removed his body cam in case he was recording. The taser, baton and cs gas all came with me, this cunt wouldn't be hurting anyone else with these weapons.

I was just about to get moving when a car screeched to a halt next to me, I grabbed the flails from my pocket and turned towards the car, fully expecting half the police station to be there for the party but it was Mark.

"Get in the car" he shouted. I just stood there looking at him "Get in the fucking car now" he screamed again. I came to my senses and moved towards the car, Mark had pushed the passenger door open, and I slumped down into the seat, closing the door as soon as my legs were in the vehicle. Mark immediately sped off, I didn't speak a word, I just sat there shaking uncontrollably as the last of the adrenaline coursed through my veins.

I finally spoke "It was him or me mate, I swear" I said, still dazed by what had just happened.

"I know kidda, I saw the whole thing" Mark replied reassuringly.

"Where are we going?" I asked.

"My house, we need to get you cleaned up and get rid of those clothes, they are covered in blood." Mark responded, as I looked down at my legs, I could see splatters of the coppers blood on my jeans.

Mark pulled over to the side of the road, now we were well away from the incident.

"Give me the weapons mate" he barked. I still wasn't thinking straight. "Give me the fucking weapons now." he shouted in my face; this snapped me back to reality and I started fumbling in my pockets for the things I had taken from the copper. Mark opened the car door and took the flails, batten, taser and gas and walked across the road, I just stared at him, not really knowing what he was doing. He dropped all the weapons down a drain at the side of the road, he struggled with the taser as it was a bit big for the grid but a couple of stamps of his foot and it went through the metal drain cover, he quickly returned to the car, almost diving in. He slammed the door shut and we sped off.

We pulled into the driveway of Marks house, and he pressed a button on a key fob attached to the car keys. The garage door sprang to life and when it was fully open Mark carefully pulled the car inside, he pressed the fob again and the garage door shut behind us. Mark said, “Stay here.” I sat in a daze on my own in the car for about a minute then Mark reappeared with a couple of bin liners and a large towel, he ordered me to get out of the car and just said “Strip”. I slowly removed each item of clothing and Mark placed them into the bin liners, I was down to just my boxers now and he handed me the towel and said, “Them too mate.”

I was now stood in marks garage naked apart from the towel covering my bottom half.

“This way.” Mark said abruptly. I followed Mark into the kitchen and almost bumped straight into his wife.

“Don’t worry darling” she said, giving me a sympathetic look as I passed her, I just nodded politely as I followed mark out into the hallway and up the stairs. Mark opened the bathroom door and pointed at the shower.

"Get cleaned dickhead." He said with a smile. I obeyed straight away, still a little dazed and shocked. I scrubbed everything that I could, paying extra attention to my face, hair and neck. I scrubbed my hands with the nail brush that was in the shower caddy hung on the wall, they were almost raw by the time I had finished. Mark appeared with a set of clothes, a T-shirt, jogging bottoms, pants and socks. I exited the shower and dried myself, Mark took the towel off me and ordered me to get dressed. I obeyed immediately.

"Downstairs" he barked, I followed him back down the stairs and along the hall into the kitchen. Marks wife had made us all a cup of tea, she offered me a shot of whiskey, but I politely declined.

"It's ok kidda, I saw everything, it was self-defense" Mark said trying to reassure me a little.

"I had no choice mate" I stammered.

"Come on and drink that tea, we need to get you home" came the blunt reply. Mark left the kitchen then returned with a pair of training shoes. "What size are you?" Mark asked,

"Twelve" I replied.

"Tough luck kidda these are an eleven, you'll have to squeeze into them" he said with a smile on his face. For some reason this made me laugh and I started to relax a little.

"Give me a minute." Mark said as he left the room. I drank the last couple of mouthfuls of tea and placed my cup on the kitchen worktop, I thanked Marks wife just as he reappeared in a sweatshirt and jogging bottoms, I just looked at him with slightly raised eyebrows.

"Our cover story dumbass, your road will be crawling with police" Mark said as he handed me a badminton racket in a case.

“I hope they don’t ask for a demonstration mate; I have never played before” I joked. Mark gave me a look of indignation and slowly shook his head. This got another little smile from me.

“We have been at the old academy school for the last hour and a half playing badminton, we had a quick glass of pop when we finished and now, I am dropping you off. Got it dickhead” Mark said. “Repeat it dumbass, where have we been?” he barked at me.

“We have been at the old academy school for the last hour and a half, we had a quick glass of pop when we finished and now, you’re dropping me off” I dutifully repeated Marks words.

“Don’t fuck up or we are both in the shit.”

“Yes dad “I said jokingly.

I said “Goodnight” to Marks wife and thanked her for her help. We exited the kitchen into the hallway and mark picked up a set of keys off the sideboard, we went out through the front door and Mark stepped aside to let me pass before shutting the door behind us. Mark pressed the key fob he had picked up and the lights flashed on his wife's car which was parked on the driveway outside the house. We both got into the small car and Mark cursed as he struggled to adjust the driver's seat into a comfortable position. The car started with a quick turn of the key and Mark reversed us off the drive, he put the car into gear, and we were off. The drive home only took about five minutes and Mark made me repeat where we had been about ten times. He had taken a massive risk for me, and I would be buying him several pints when we got the chance.

As we entered my road, we saw blue lights everywhere. Mark slowly drove down the road and pulled into a parking space about twenty meters from my house. As soon as we stopped two policy enforcement officers headed towards the car. "Don't fuck up son;" Mark said as I exited the vehicle.

I put my hand up to Mark as I shut the door and said "Good game mate, I'll see you next week" through the open car window. I was clutching one of the rackets Mark had given me and the other was on the back seat of the car along with a tatty sports bag Mark had thrown in for effect.

"Excuse me sir" came the officer's voice whilst gesturing to Mark to stay still.

"Yes mate, what's up?" I replied as naturally as I could.

"Can I ask where you have been tonight?" the officer enquired.

"Just been to badminton mate, why what`s up?" I asked. The second copper was now at Marks window, probably asking the same question.

"A police officer has been attacked by what we believe to be two or three men, just down from the church around the corner. We are just asking about to see if anyone saw or heard anything?" came the officer's reply.

"Sorry mate but we have been out for about two hours. When did this happen?" I asked politely.

"About nine thirty sir." The officer replied. ""Sorry mate but we were just finishing our game then." I lied convincingly.

"Well, if you do hear anything please contact your local station." The copper nodded politely as he spoke.

"No problem, mate, will do. "I said. The second officer had finished with mark and had stepped back onto the curb. I leant down and put my hand out to mark through the open window, as I shook his hand I said, "Cheers mate, see you next week." Mark nodded as he put the car into gear and pulled away. The officers were now heading down the road towards the turning for the church. I retrieved the house keys from the pocket on the jogging bottoms and headed for the front door, the keys were the only original possession I had left the house with earlier, everything else had been bagged up at Marks.

I put the familiar shaped key into the front door lock, turned it and pushed the door open, I stepped in and closed the door, reached up and threw the bolt across. I breathed a sigh of relief as I kicked the undersized trainers off and placed the badminton racket onto the table as I made my way toward the stairs. I quietly climbed the stairs and went straight into my room to change into a fresh set my own clothes before popping my head around the door of my lad's room. "Alright son?" I asked.

"Shhh I'm in a game." Came the familiar reply. I could have walked in covered in blood and he wouldn't have noticed. I headed back along the landing then down the stairs straight into the kitchen and grabbed a beer from the fridge. I turned the lamp on in the lounge then slumped heavily into the settee. Now I could start to process what happened tonight.

I replayed the events in my head over and over for an hour, and concluded it was self-defense. The copper had jumped out and started harassing me, I had committed no crime, so I had no business with him. He didn't like this so he became aggressive, I did nothing wrong, and the cunt shot me with his taser gun, he could have killed me stone dead and got away with it just because it's his job, well fuck him, my job is to get back home safely to my lad and I'm not letting some jumped up little unimportant prick stop me from doing that. The fake authority he believed he had, had gone to this cunts head. Decent, hardworking men and women have the right to defend themselves regardless of who the attacker is, and these corporate bully boys are terrified of the day we all realize it. I took a huge swig of beer and tried to put it out of my mind, but I know I have a sleepless night ahead of me.

My thoughts drifted to the GoPro camera, I panicked a little bit, but then calmed myself as I remembered picking it up with all the other stuff," Mark must still have it at his house," I thought, I know he will get rid of the clothes, but I don't know about the camera. I can't just message him as it will incriminate him if anything happens. I let out a deep sigh and thought "Whatever will be will be." I drank the last of my beer, turned the lamp off and headed upstairs to bed.

6

"Your ignorance is their power."

The alarm clock buzzed into life at ten past six, but I had been awake most of the night. I fumbled with the button to silence it, throwing back the covers I swung my legs out of the bed and onto the carpeted floor. I dressed quickly and headed for the bathroom, I used the loo, washed my face and brushed my teeth before heading to my lad's room to try and wake him, getting the usual grunts in return for my efforts. I made my way downstairs and into the kitchen, I flicked the kettle on and dropped two pieces of bread into the toaster. Last night's events were still going through my mind as the bread slowly turned to toast and the kettle spewed steam as it reached the boil. I carried my completed breakfast into the lounge and slumped down onto the settee,

I was eating on autopilot as my mind was preoccupied with the copper's attack from last night. I glanced at the clock on the wall, it was six twenty-eight, so I stood up and went back to the kitchen and plugged the radio in. At six thirty the news came on and I was hoping to hear about last night's events.

The news started with the usual nonsense, the politicians had awarded themselves another pay rise, the nurses had been screwed over again by the politicians and some parasites had increased the polices powers to harass the unvaccinated, then the one I had been waiting for. The news readers somber and serious voice started. "And finally, a police officer was seriously hurt and left with head injuries last night in Bloxton, when he was attacked by a group of men, according to an eyewitness who was attending a local church, three men attacked the police officer, and after beating him unconscious, stole his weapons. A spokesperson for the local police confirmed that an officer remains in a critical condition and it's too early to say whether the officer has any permanent damage caused by his injuries. Police are urging any witnesses to contact Bloxton police station."

"Fuck him" I said as I flicked the switch to turn the radio off. I said a silent "thankyou" to the eyewitness who said there were three attackers. I headed back upstairs and woke my lad up, making sure he sat up in bed and wouldn't close his eyes and nod off again. "I am off to work now mate, I'll see you later, love you" I said as I was leaving the room. I got the usual grunt in response but at least I tried.

I returned to the lounge and sat on the settee to lace my work boots up, I grabbed the van keys, dug the phone out of the metal tin in the drawer and powered it up and pocketed some cash before heading out the front door to load the van with some power tools. I had already seen the policy enforcement officer approaching as I made my first trip to the van, I had gone back into the house and picked up two more toolboxes before taking a deep breath and heading back out.

“Excuse me sir” the officer said as he approached.

“Yes mate” came my polite response.

“There was a serious attack on a police constable just around the corner last night at around nine thirty, and I am just asking people if they heard or saw anything?” The copper continued.

I wanted to say “If he was acting as a police constable and enforcing common law he would be ok, but he was playing the role of policy enforcement officer and he was a cunt” but that would of got me in the shit so I politely said “No sorry mate, I have already spoke to an officer last night, I had been out playing badminton and I missed all the excitement.”

“I would hardly call it excitement sir; a police officer was seriously hurt.” He protested.

“Sorry officer I missed all the commotion.” I replied. The officer turned on his heels and walked away.

I locked the front door and got into the van. My thoughts kept going back to the events of last night and every time I ran through it, I came to the same conclusion, “It was him or me so fuck him.”

The harassment during the day was decreasing slightly, in the past six months the policy enforcement officers had been stopping people all the time, but the people were wising up on how to deal with them. keeping the doors locked on the cars and only speaking through a slightly opened window was a favorite or just holding up a handwritten sign with “No because of covid” on it was another way or “No I am protecting my family.” was another method. If only the people knew that they had no business with these parasites if they had committed no crime. For there to be a crime there must be a victim, but just going about your daily business and being harassed was the real crime. We are under no lawful obligation to even speak to them if we haven't done anything wrong. They trick us into doing business by getting us to give a legal name, if we don't refuse, but ask if we are obliged to give a name, the answer should be "No you're not obliged." Then if we ask, am I being charged with a crime, and if we haven't committed a crime then the answer should be "No you're not being charged with a crime." Then we ask if we're free to go and the answer should be "Yes, you're free to go. "

My day at work was pretty uneventful, but time had dragged on as I couldn't get the images of the copper's face out of my head. I just kept saying "Fuck him." Under my breath.

I needed to go shopping, but because I had forgotten about the unvaccinated only being allowed in the supermarkets on Wednesdays, my best option was the smaller shops, but I pulled up on the supermarket car park anyway. I checked for my bank card in the little slot in my phone case, exited the van and pressed the key fob to lock the doors. As I walked across the car park, I kept an eye out for the policy enforcement officers, but I couldn't see any. I marched straight through the doors of the supermarket into the foyer. The security guard looked up briefly from his bank of screens but took no notice of me, I found this strange, but it soon became apparent why.

Just inside the doors were two PCSO`s, one male and one female, both looking ridiculous in their ill-fitting uniforms. I walked right between them, just as the male PCSO was raising his hand in protest I raised my hand and said, "Not today thank you." They both immediately set off after me.

"Excuse me sir;" The female one said loudly and a little perturbed by my lack of respect for their imaginary authority.

I didn't reply in the way she was expecting, and this really annoyed her. "Sir!! Sir!! are you implying I have legal title young lady?" I replied trying to stifle a laugh.

"I am erm, I erm." She stammered.

"Are you implying I have legal tittle?" I repeated and she didn't know what to say.

"We have the authority." The male one started to speak but I cut him off.

"No that's not true, the only authority you have is the authority you have given yourselves, and I don't stand under your authority. Now I am a busy man so if you don't mind, I will continue getting my shopping." I replied sternly. They both went into stuttering and stammering mode with lots of "We have`s." and "The powers granted." I just looked at them with contempt and said, "Leave me alone or I will be arresting you two for breaching my peace." With this a small round of applause broke out from the small crowd of onlookers that had gathered to watch the spectacle. The two PCSO`s returned to their perch by the door to wait for an easier victim and I continued with my shopping, unvaccinated, unchecked and smiling from ear to ear.

A few of the onlookers said, "Well done." And "Good on you mate." As I passed them further along the isle`s. I thought to myself "This is what the people need to do, just stand up for themselves and say "no." With a full trolley and a smile, I exited the supermarket, bidding the PCSO`s "Good evening." On the way out. The male one just looked away and the female one glared at me with hatred in her eyes. No laws were broken, and no crime was committed so I had no business with them, simple as that.

7

"Stay patient and trust your journey."

My day at work passed without incident and being a Friday, we finished a little earlier than normal. As I got close to home, I got caught in traffic, which was very unusual for this stretch of road, despite being the main route through town. At first, I thought it was an accident but after opening the van door and standing up on the sill I could see the problem. Policy enforcement officers were blocking the road and harassing people, probably manufacturing their victim's consent to do business. The poor uneducated victims were probably giving their legal names which straight away made them open for business, I mean why go out chasing criminals for zero profit when you can unlawfully give out fines and top up the pension pot.

I sat back down in the van and got comfy, I put my seat belt back on and ensured all the doors were locked by pressing the button on the dashboard. I was still about ten cars away from the roadblock, there were no side roads to turn down and the section of road they had chosen had a central barrier to prevent u turns. I had no choice but to wait my turn to be harassed. As I got closer to the front of the que, I felt the familiar rush of adrenaline start to fill my veins. I can clearly see what they are up to now, they are checking the carbon output of people's cars and fining people who aren't up to date with the footprint payments. It's the latest load of money-making bollocks from the climate agenda. Your phone data is used to track your mileage and a fine is given out for excessive vehicle use. I discreetly reach into the leg pocket of my work trousers and retrieve my phone, I press and hold the button on the side of the phone and the power off symbol flashes up on the screen, I press the symbol and the screen goes blank as the phone shuts down, I then drop the phone between the seats.

The car in front pulls away and it's my turn to be harassed, so I slowly pull forward until I am in the trap. I look at the policy enforcement officer standing with his hand in the air indicating for me to stop, and I recognize him as the partner of WPC fat arse from earlier in the week. "This should be fun." I thought to myself as I pulled the window down just enough to hear and be heard.

"Good afternoon, sir" the young copper said with an air of confidence.

"I am not a sir constable, are you acting on your oath today?" I replied bluntly.

"I erm, what do you mean?" came the confused response.

"You took an oath to the king to uphold the laws of the land and cause the peace to be kept, I was just wondering if you are keeping the peace now constable or are you forcing the policies of the corporate government onto people?" I replied, trying not to smile as a look of confusion crossed his young face.

"Sir I don't know what you are on about." He answered as a frown appeared on his forehead. "Why have you stopped me constable?" I asked the worried looking copper.

"I am checking for excessive millage of the people in the vehicles on this road sir." he said almost apologetically.

"Again constable, you have addressed me as sir and I have no legal title, I am just a man. Now if you are not charging me with a crime am I free to go?" I replied, always answering a question with a question.

"You are not being charged with a crime, but I need to see your mobile phone Mr.?" He tried again.

"Am I obliged to give you a name constable?" again I answered a question with a question. “Yes, sir you are obliged when a police officer asks you” He either lied or didn’t know the truth.

“I will ask you again constable am I, a man, obliged to give you a name?” I replied, staring directly into his eyes. He was now looking around for help as most people fell for his tricks and played along but not me, I stood my ground.

“Sarge” the officer shouted. I turned my head to look slightly back over my right shoulder and saw a stocky man in his late forty’s approaching my van.

“What’s wrong?” the sergeant asked the younger copper.

“This man keeps saying he’s not a sir and he doesn’t have to give me his name.” the younger copper blurted.

“We will see about that?” the sergeant said. “Good day sir.” The sergeant said politely.

"As I told the constable, sergeant I am not a sir as I have no legal title. Now let's start with your name and number?" I demanded as I reached over and retrieved a pen from the dashboard. "It's sergeant Richards, number six zero zero four and what's your name sir, sorry mate?" he responded.

"I don't use names sergeant, and what station are you from?" I replied answering a question with a question.

"Bloxton station." Came the blunt response. "And who's the duty inspector, sergeant?" I asked.

"There's no need for all that mate, you are free to go." Sergeant Richards said as he motioned with his hand for me to leave.

"But serge." The young constable started to protest but the sergeant raised his hand and silenced him.

I drove off smiling to myself "That's another little victory for decent men and women." I thought as I headed down the road in the direction of home. I pulled into my road and just for a change I was able to park right outside my house, I turned the engine off and took the house keys out of the little tray on the dashboard, after unloading a few power tools into the house I was about to take my boots off when the door knocked, which was unusual as most of my visitors came by invitation. As I headed for the door, I glanced into the little mirror I had positioned on a shelf next to the window its angled to get a look at any visitors and to my surprise, stood at my door was the young copper from earlier. I hesitated, and thought "Do I pretend not to be in and hope he goes away or answer and see what he wants?" As I hadn't done anything wrong, I chose to answer, but first I checked I could reach my baseball bat in case I needed it. I wrapped my left hand around the wooden handle on the bat and cautiously opened the door with my right hand. If for any reason, he rushed the door I would step aside and give him the bat full force across the head. My left foot acted as a door stop and only allowed the door to open a short way.

"Yes constable?" I asked through the gap in the door.

"You don't need to do all that mate; I just want to talk to you." He replied.

"Well, I'm not sure I have anything to say to you constable." I replied cautiously.

"My radio, camera and taser are all in the car. I did a PCN check on your van and got your address," He continued "It's the second time we have crossed paths this week and both times you have walked away without giving your details, I have only been a constable for about three months, and I just wanted to know what you are doing?" he said inquisitively.

"All I am doing is standing up for truth and honesty constable. As men and women, we are under no obligation to do business with you or the corporation you work for, when you are acting in your fictional capacity as a policy enforcement officer, trying to manufacture our consent, so you can enforce the statutes, acts and mandates of this corrupt and treasonous government onto us. Did they not teach you the difference between common law, the law of the land and statute law constable?" I replied.

"Erm no but what does it mean?" He replied. "It means you took an oath to uphold the common laws of this land and not the rules of the corporation that is calling itself government. The government is a corporation constable, and the police forces are corporations. When you are forcing the rules of the government corporation onto men and women then you are not acting as a constable but a policy enforcement officer. We are governed and policed by consent, and as long as we have committed no crime, that is caused harm, loss or defrauded another man or woman then we have the right to withdraw our consent to be harassed with these corporate rules. If I had hurt someone, I would hold my hands up and say "Fair play" but if there is no victim there is no crime. What you will be doing for most of your career is manufacturing peoples consent to do business with the unlawful administrative courts, tricking people into contracting with you, and handing out fines to make money for another corporation, they have monetized sin constable, and you are the delivery man for the unlawful courts. Now if you will excuse me, I must prepare tea for me and my son, I suggest you do a little research constable and find out just what it is they have you doing." I replied.

"My name is Stuart" he said almost apologetically.

"Well Stuart, I don't use names. Now research what I told you." I replied.

"Thank you, I will" with that he turned and walked off and I shut the door. I immediately thought "If we can educate them maybe they will realize what they are doing."

8

"The power of the people is stronger than the people in power."

The alarm buzzed loudly, and I rolled over and squinted at the clock, it was six forty am, I threw the covers back and heaved myself up then turned the alarm off. I headed to the bathroom and completed the usual morning ablutions still trying to shake the sleep from my body. I returned to the bedroom, dressed quickly and headed for the kitchen. The kettle crackled into life, and I placed two rounds of bread into the toaster. There are a bunch of us heading for the city today to attend a freedom rally in the main square. The policy enforcement officers will be out in force using their bully boy tactics and suppressing the truth and free speech, but we outnumber them ten to one. The plans for this were made months ago and only spread through word of mouth. The days of text messaging a friend with this sort of info have long gone and most people won't even bring phones with them. The need for the sneaky meetings and passing pieces of paper from man to man arose from the constant monitoring of all electronic devices and arrests for anyone spreading the truth. Lots of good people are risking their freedom to stand up to the fake authorities and today is an important day.

The kettle clicks as it turns off and I pour the boiling water over the instant coffee in my mug, the nicely toasted bread pops out of the toaster, and I quickly smear a layer of butter then jam onto it. I sit quietly eating my breakfast and going through different scenarios in my head "What if this happens?" and "What if that happens?" I think to myself as I plan different responses to all the possible outcomes of standing up to these tyrants. In the end I just think

"Fuck it I will do what I need to do at the time."

It was seven thirty when I left the house, I had cash on me but no bank cards, phone or anything to identify me. I have a new GoPro camera which is fully charged tucked away in my coat pocket. I carefully hid my house keys under a rock behind the bush at the front of the house, following advice I received from a friend. It seems the policy enforcement officers have been letting themselves into the houses of people they have arrested, without getting a warrant. They get your address and whilst you are being unlawfully detained, and if you have keys on you, they help themselves, sometimes planting listening devices and sometimes drugs or other incriminating evidence.

There is a train station within walking distance, but the police will be on the platform harassing people who they suspect of heading for the rally, as despite our best efforts to keep things secret, some people have big mouths, so I place a silly cloth mask on my face, and I jump on the bus instead. I pay my fare then move along the aisle until I find an empty seat. I recognize about twenty people on the bus, and I know they are heading for the rally. I take my seat and settle in for the journey. Any of the faces I don't recognize could be plain clothed policemen just trying to pick up information. We are all well drilled in their sneaky tactics, so we all sit quietly and don't acknowledge each other. The ones that do talk discuss football and other trivial matters, but nobody mentions the rally.

As the bus makes each stop, and people get onboard, I recognize more faces mixed in with the shoppers and commuters. Most of the people are heading for the rally. We are less than two miles from the city center and the traffic starts to slow to a crawl. I move my head to the right to see past the man seated in front of me, and I can see the reason for the slow traffic, about ten cars down is a police roadblock. They are probably checking identification cards or vaccine statuses on phones, and just generally harassing innocent people.

The officers wave a few cars through, the occupants are probably elderly or families that they don't see as a threat. Another couple of vehicles then it's our turn. The van in front of us stops and a copper opens the back to reveal a few battered old tools and a step ladder, he quickly closes the rear doors and signals to his college to let the van go. Now it's our turn. The bus driver opens the doors, and a rush of cool air enters the bus accompanied by the mechanical swoosh sound of the doors opening. Two policy enforcement officers enter the bus and immediately start trying to intimidate people, the taller of the two speaks first "Right then ladies and gents, who is heading for this illegal rally then?" He is met with complete silence, even the shoppers and commuters are fed up with being harassed, and they remain silent. He turns toward the nearest passenger,

"Identification and vaccine status?" comes the blunt request.

"Am I obliged to obey you constable?" the man replies. I try and stop myself from smiling. Knowledge is power and it appears everyone is learning to deal with these parasites.

"When a police officer asks for your identification, you are supposed to show him." The copper tries again.

"Let's start with your name and number constable, that is if you are acting as a police constable today and not a policy enforcement officer?" the man answered a question with a question.

"I am a police officer, and you will show me some respect, do you understand?" the copper snarled as he spoke.

"I don't understand or stand under your authority officer, now are you here on your oath today?" the man answers with a question again.

“I am here doing my job, and I will do it however I like;” the officer exclaimed almost shouting. “Now show me some identification.” He barked again.

“Are you asking me to falsely label myself officer?” the man replied, stifling a smile.

“I don’t know what you mean sir.” The copper protested.

“ID means false and entification means giving objective existence to something, so are you asking me to provide ID-entification officer?” the man responded with a question. The officer’s blood was really boiling now, and the man just sat there cool as you like, ready to answer a question with a question,

“Give me your name now.” The officer demanded.

“Am I obliged to give you a name?” came his quick reply. At this the officer gave up on this man and tried another victim.

This time it was a younger man in his mid-twenties at a guess. "This could be interesting. I wonder if the younger generation have realized that you don't have to do business with these people if you have done nothing wrong." I thought as the copper got in the young man's face.

"You, name?" was the blunt question from the copper.

"Let's start with your name, number and your duty inspectors name constable, contact him on your radio and tell him there has been a trespass, and I am holding him accountable;" The young man exclaimed with confidence. The officer was boiling at this point and moved on to another potential victim.

"You, show me some ID." The agitated officer barked at a man a few seats away.

"No." the man replied bluntly. Now this was a mistake, as you can't refuse, you can only ask if you're obliged, and as you're not obligated to give a name you don't own then they have to say you're not obliged. "Are you refusing sir?" the officer replied, realizing he had found his victim. "I don't have to show you anything, now go away;" the man exclaimed. The other policy enforcement officer moved forward and took the man by the arm.

"Come with me sir." The officer said as he pulled the man up from his seat. He led the man along the aisle towards the front of the bus and out through the door onto the pavement. "You all think you're very clever don't you, but he wasn't so smart was he? We will win in the end;" the arrogant coppers accomplice sneered as he walked along the bus and out onto the pavement to join his colleague and the man.

I watched through the window as the scene unfolded outside. The man who was removed from the bus had reached into his jacket and had shown the two officers something, they both immediately backed off slightly, the officer who asked all the questions on the bus gestured for the man to leave and reboard the bus. Now the only thing that would get you released that quick is a warrant card and that would explain why the man unwittingly gave the wrong answers and got dragged off in the first place. He was one of them and didn't know what to say.

I wasn't the only one to notice this either. A few of us were exchanging glances and nodding at each other. The man reboarded the bus and started to make his way back to his seat. "Morning officer." The first victim of the uniformed officer said as the undercover copper walked past. The copper shot a stare at the man and didn`t know whether to turn around and get off or continue to his seat.

. "Come and take a seat officer." The man in the seat behind where the copper had been sitting said as he patted the cushion on the empty chair. "Are you here on your oath today constable?" another voice boomed from the back of the bus. The look on the coppers face was priceless, and he just stared forward as the bus pulled off.

I glanced back towards the visibly frightened copper and saw some of the men behind him passing a luminous sticker along the bus with the word police on it in black letters. The man directly behind the copper peeled the paper off the back to reveal the sticky pad, and with a gentle pat on the back the sticker was applied. "Never mind constable, better luck next time." the man said as he patted the ununiformed coppers back, discreetly applying the sticker as he did so.

The stickers were a tactic we used with people we suspected of being policy enforcers. They were patted on the back and labeled as police for the benefit of the decent people around them. The officer was oblivious to the sticker and continued to nervously stare forward. The man behind him reached up and rang the bell for the bus to stop. "Isn`t this your stop constable?" he questioned with a smile.

With this the undercover copper stood up and headed for the exit, as the bus slowed down everyone on the bus let out an almighty cheer.

There was no need for any violence as the dent to the officer's pride was enough. The bus came to a halt and as the officer exited another cheer went up, and in fairness to him he just shrugged his shoulders, turned and smiled at us and said, "Maybe next time lads;" Another roar went up from the men on the bus and I even caught a glimpse of the bus driver smiling in the rear-view mirror.

As we approached the bus terminal, which is located only a couple of hundred meters from the main square where the rally was taking place, I felt a pang of excitement in my stomach. As usual at these events I had nothing unlawful on me, no weapons or identification. I had a baseball cap on that could be tilted down to stop the facial recognition cameras, a brand-new go pro camera in my jacket and one hundred pounds cash in my pocket, other than that just the clothes on my back and my walking boots.

The bus came to a halt in the terminal, and with a loud hiss the front suspension lowered, and the doors opened. I could clearly see there was a large police presence around the terminus, and as we headed towards the front of the bus a handful of policy enforcement officers headed over towards us. One policy officer had a camera and was filming us as we exited the bus. I reached into my jacket pocket and retrieved the GoPro camera; I pressed the button on top of the little device, and it beeped into life.

I raised the camera to eye level to block my face and pointed it straight into the face of the copper with the camera, who was now within touching distance.

"What are you doing with that?" he barked.

"Gathering evidence for the trials for when this is over;" I replied with a smile. As I moved forward, I rotated with the little camera to keep it pointed at the copper's face and this prevented him from getting a clear picture of me. When I was far enough away, he turned the camera onto another man from the bus, the man just raised his hand and blocked the copper from filming.

We all headed in different directions and my plan was just to circle around and head back to the square via another route. I walked into a department store and did a bit of browsing before leaving by another exit on the right of the store. I bought a bottle of water from a little news kiosk and put it into one of the pockets on my jacket, saving it for later. Another makeshift stall was selling a variety of hats with football badges on them amongst other things, so I picked up a plain black wooly hat, paid the vendor and carried on. The hat would come in handy later if I needed a quick change of appearance.

With just a few more twists and turns I was back on the main street that led to the square. There were copper's everywhere and most of them had riot gear with them, we had come for a peaceful rally and to hear some truth being spoken and this lot had come for violence. I already knew there would be plain clothed police mingling with us and trying to get the crowd revved up to fight but we had a way of dealing with them.

I was now no more than twenty meters away from the main square , the weather was unusually warm for a Septembers day but I put it down to the skies being sprayed again to push the climate change agenda, "It's easier to fool the people than to convince the people they are being fooled" I thought to myself then remembered the climate change rally two weeks earlier had been allowed to go ahead with hardly any police presence and no arrests. Strange how people speaking the truth and fighting for freedom are harassed and people pushing the latest money-making scam are allowed to do what they want. This is what happens when you go against the official narrative. They don't want you thinking for yourself, they just want you to believe their latest fear-mongering exercise and give them more money to sort out the problem they have created.

My thoughts were disturbed by the sight that greeted me as I entered the square. My jaw dropped as I looked around, there were hundreds if not several thousand people, all races, colors and creeds. Men and women with one thing in common and that was freedom from the oppressive government nonsense. There was no loud shouting or pushing and shoving, just decent people gathering together.

As I made my way through the crowd, I had people handing me leaflets and with just a quick glance I could see bits of the information we had been gathering was printed on them. A smile crept across my face as it dawned on me that we were growing in numbers, and the information needed to beat these parasites was starting to be spread freely, people didn't give a damn now, we were at the very cusp of revolution. The people were waking up and about to take back their power.

There were people laughing and joking and music was coming from the main stage, which was just the back of a rigid lorry with the curtain sides pulled back. The smell of hot dogs and burgers filled the air as the fast-food vendors that were regulars in the square did a roaring trade with the people in the crowd. I continued making my way through the crowd and with a few "Excuse me's." and "Can I squeeze through please mate." I got to where I was heading.

"Alright Dan?" said a friendly voice.

"How's it going?" I replied,

"Not so bad mate, it's a good turn out." My friend gestured towards the crowd with his hand.

"Not half mate, have you read some of the leaflets going about?" I enquired.

"I've had a quick glance, but I'll read them later." My mate replied.

The music stopped and the sound of a microphone giving feedback filled the square. Almost immediately the crowd fell silent, and all eyes were on the makeshift stage. A man who appeared to be in his fifties was tapping the microphone, and after clearing his throat he started to address the crowd. "Ladies and gentlemen, men and women, freedom fighters. I would like to thank you all for coming today."

As he started a cheer went up from the crowd and a huge round of applause swept through the square. "I would like to thank the organizers of this little get together and a big thanks' for a certain friend for the loan of the lorry and sound equipment that is making this possible." With this another huge cheer of appreciation swept through the crowd. The man was now gesturing with his hand for people to quieten down so he could continue. "Just a few things before we start today, please remember that this is a peaceful meeting to share information and not an excuse for violence or for damage to persons or property." He looked directly at the large number of policy enforcement officers that had gathered on the outskirts of the square as he said this.

"Any violence will result in citizens arrests being made and a common law court will be convened, and the true law of the land being enforced" he continued. With this most of the crowd turned and faced the gathering of coppers who were growing in number at the back of the square. "Are you here on your oaths today constables?" he shouted into the mike "I trust that you will be keeping the peace today and not forcing the statutes, acts and mandates of this corrupt and treasonous government onto us men and women?" he said lightheartedly. This got another cheer from the crowd and the speaker continued. "Ladies and gentlemen, boys and girls and our police constables, I know you want to hear our first guest speaker so without further ado, I am pleased to introduce the chief constable of West Mainland police," his voice tailed off as the crowd booed and hissed. "Only joking, our first guest is no stranger to most of you and a true man in every sense of the word, I am pleased to welcome onto the stage John of the family Wright." With this the crowd erupted into cheers and applause.

This man's knowledge was excellent, and he had many victories against the corrupt authorities under his belt. The crowd started to quiet down, and all eyes and ears were focused on the man who had entered the stage.

"Good day, truth seekers." Another cheer went up as he began to speak then a respectful silence descended on the square. "As you know, I John, a man, have been fighting for our freedoms for a number of years now, with some success and some failures. I, like you, just want to be left in peace and be able to live a good life without being forced to obey the rules and regulations of a bunch of self-serving parasites" he continued "I want my children, grandchildren and all future generations to be free men and women, not slaves or chattel as they are now. It is with knowledge of the tricks and treachery of these so-called elites and ruling classes that we, the good men and women of the world can fight for our freedoms. We have the right to say no to the money-making rules, disguised as laws, and a huge no to filth being injected into our bodies, so I thought I would start today by discussing consent. You are under no lawful obligation to consent to the statutes, acts or mandates of the corporation that is government. You are under no lawful obligation to obey the statutes, acts and mandates of the corporation that is calling itself government. You have the right to remove your consent to be governed. The rules they have made are manmade, therefore beneath man, and as men and women you do not have to consent to the rules of another man or woman, and as long as you haven't committed a crime, and for there to be a crime then there must be a victim, someone must have suffered harm, loss, damage or been defrauded by you, if you haven't committed a crime then you can remove your consent. Now I know all of you here obey the common law, which is the law of the land or god's law. Now we are trying to educate you about the rules of these corporations masquerading as laws. Have you noticed how they have a rule for everything, and if you break their rules, you must give them money? All they have done is monetized sin and when they make everything a sin they make money, now do you get it?" John paused for a second or two to let his words sink in and a few shouts and cheers came up from the crowd.

I glanced around to see what the coppers were doing and realized some of them were actually listening to the man's words. "Education and information are what these policy enforcement officers need." I thought to myself.

John continued “You can remove your consent at any time by saying no thankyou I am withdrawing my consent, it is not just a woman’s right to remove consent for sex at any time, it is every man and woman’s right to say no consent to any man-made nonsense.”

With this a huge cheer went up, this is what these men and women needed, just information and education. “This subject goes very deep,” john continued “When a policy enforcement officer asks you for your name, that is the name that you have been led to believe is you, he is trying to manufacture your consent to do business with him, and by giving the name, notice I said the name and not your name, you are giving him or her joinder. Stop using legal names, stop answering to the name MR JOHN SMITH or MRS JANE JONES. Stop being a name, you are men and women, you are dad, son, brother, sister, aunties, uncles but you are not a fictional name. This will take a bit more explaining, lads and lasses. For example, when you give the legal fiction name, I will say it again, the legal fiction name, for example MR JOHN SMITH or MRS JANE JONES, you are committing crown copyright theft, and that is what gives the policy enforcement officer the excuse to do what he wants with you."

I glanced around at the boys in blue and saw a few open mouths as the words sank in. I know John is watering this speech down a bit and it will take a lot more research, but as a starting point this information is excellent.

"You are not obliged to give a name as the police officer cannot ask you to commit a crime, you are you, and the police officer is him or her" another huge cheer went up from the crowd. "Start to learn how to deal with this fake authority, start to stand up for yourselves, start to realize the wool has been pulled over your eyes and start to educate yourselves" John was getting going now.

"We as men and women have the right to share this knowledge, and not only the right but a duty to share the knowledge, we have the right to be here, now today, we have a right to say yes and no as we see fit, and we don't have to obey the nonsense of a bunch of self-serving parasitic, treasonous tyrants. If we do not stand up for our rights, then we will lose those rights. Even as we speak, they are making more rules to stop freedom of speech and freedom of information. They are trying to tax the air you breathe and when that fails, they will tax your emissions. Everyone here will have witnessed them blocking information on social media platforms, using so called fact checkers, these people are truth blockers and disinformation spreaders; The truth is of no use to these people as it disrupts their lies." Another huge cheer went up, and a quick glance around from me revealed a few confused coppers.

John looked into the eyes of several people as he took a few breaths then continued. "I cannot fit a life time's worth of information into one short speech to make you truly free, but if you only take a few words away with you today , then let these words be firstly , no consent, and why, ask why every time an unlawful fine drops through your door onto your mat, ask why every time a new rule is made up , ask why every time someone with imaginary authority tries to do business with you. The system is a scam based on your consent, you are tricked into consenting to be governed by registering to vote , you are tricked into doing business with the private security companies trading as policy enforcement organizations, you are tricked into doing business with the courts which are private corporations, not interested in justice but in love with profits, your even tricked into giving ownership of your car to them, what about your kids? Anybody registered their child's birth; well Regis is the crown and anything you register, you abandon, and they claim. Please look deeper?"

The crowd erupted into cheers and applause, shouts of "more john, more john." Swept through the square. I was surprised the police hadn’t tried to shut the rally down, but I think the information they were hearing was starting to sink in with them. We had a right to be here, and they knew it. The crowd settled down and John began to speak again.

“Thank you for your support and the kind applause. With the correct information we can stop these tyrants. Who here votes?” John asked, a few hands went up, and immediately the crowd turned and stared at the voters. “Who registers to vote?” John asked whilst scanning the crowd for raised hands. This time a few more hands went up. “Then you have consented to be governed.” He said with a sigh. “Who doesn’t even fill the form out?” The crowd cheered loudly and nearly every hand in the crowd was raised. “Well, your silence is your consent” Every hand came down and people were exchanging confused glances. “They have you one way or another. If you fill the form out you consented to be governed, and if you don’t fill the form out, they send another form that says if all the information is correct, then you don't need to do anything, and of course when you read the form it has the legal fiction name on it, MR JOHN SMITH or MRS JANE JONES and by doing nothing, you have consented. This time the crowd was silent.

"Anybody here registered their car with the devious vehicle licensing agency?" most of the hands in the crowd went up. "Well, anything you register or regis-ster, you give legal title of it to the crown, Regis is the crown, this includes your car, your children and even your right to vote." The stunned silence spoke volumes, you could almost see the cogs turning in the heads of the men and women in the crowd. Could this be true, that doing what we have been taught is the right thing to do and registering things we are actually giving them away?

"Don't be angry with yourselves, you only did what you were tricked into doing, it's not your fault. Think about it, if they didn't own your car by tricking you into giving it to them, then they couldn't charge you for the use of it and they definitely couldn't tow it away and crush it, because that would be theft and criminal damage? But if you registered it with them then they can do whatever they like as its theirs. Start to wake up people, you are being conned. I want you to leave here today with a list of words to think about, a few ideas and concepts to take with you and research and work on. I want you to spread the word, tell your neighbors, family members and your friends. I want you to educate your children, because a child only educated in the public school system is fully indoctrinated and not educated. I am sure some of you have recorded my little talk here today, and I'm sure you will post it on any media platform that you can, for that you have my blessing. The fact that we haven't been shut down yet means someone or some people want to hear what we are saying, so here are some words for you to research, coercion, force, registration, lawful meaning of license. I want you to research consent, honor and dishonor, in fact I want you to research every single thing you can about the scams and treachery of the parasites who believe they have power over us. You are being conned with language and bullshit, and remember no consent, and ask why? Thank you, you've been a fantastic audience." John finished talking and the crowd erupted into a huge round of applause.

The weather was still nice for September and despite the heat I kept the cap on my head to protect my face from the cameras that were all over the square. I took the water bottle from my jacket pocket, unscrewed the lid and took several big gulps of the now slightly tepid water. A man walked past and handed out more leaflets, I took a couple and folded them up and put them in my pocket. The square was filled with music now from the sound system on the stage as the next speaker was still preparing to talk. I took the opportunity to have a good look at the boys in blue who were being quite friendly for a change, all I could think was it must be the calm before the storm.

It suddenly dawned on me that there was no longer any need to sneak about with bits of information on pieces of paper or strange meetings with people in parks. The information we had been gathering and worrying about being caught with had just been broadcast to several hundred if not thousands of people, all of which would probably share it with thousands more people, it would be all over social media later and as fast as the fact checkers could make up lies about it, the truth would be reposted and spread.

I smiled to myself as I realized the importance of today, it's a turning point, a new time where people can start to wake up and hopefully a time of peace.

Some of the information given by the speakers today will free us from the tyranny of this treasonous government and some of the information will free us from the money-making scams of the policy enforcement officers and the unlawful administrative courts. Above all the information will allow us to take back control of our lives by removing the illusion of power theses Muppets have and making us realize we are men and women not bloody slaves to a man-made system.

I glanced around at the faces of the men and women and I could physically feel the energy starting to build up in the square, there were men and women from all walks of life who were fed up of being told what to do by criminals masquerading as government, they were sick of being bullied by university graduates that relied not on strength or ability to enforce unjust laws but instead they relied on the fact you couldn't fight back through fear of imprisonment by some corrupt judge.

The sun was beating down now, and the square was filled with a warm light that was adding to the energy and mood of the men and women gathered here today, only the odd passing cloud cast a slight shadow on the event. The smell of fast food was in the air and although I was tempted, I refrained from going in search of the delights of the burger or hot dog stands, settling instead for another mouthful of water.

The music was interrupted by the voice of the man introducing the guests as the microphone crackled into life. “Ladies and gentlemen, policy enforcement officers and genuine police constables,” the announcer got a little cheer from the crowd and with a quick look over my shoulder I could see even a few of the coppers were smiling. “We have our next speaker here with us today. This young lady has studied her subject for a while now and with her excellent delivery technique I am sure you will leave here enlightened, so without further ado please put your hands together for Sarah.” The crowd cheered loudly at the mention of this name and although I had read bits of her work, I had not studied it in any great depth.

“Good afternoon sovereign men and women” Sarah started speaking and the crowd gave a welcoming cheer. “It’s lovely to be here on this sunny Saturday, I would like to start todays talk with some information regarding article sixty-one, now some of you may know this already but some of you won’t so I will break it down into the basics and then you can go off and research it for yourself.” The crowd kept a respectful silence whilst Sarah spoke.

“Under article sixty-one of the magna carta of 1215, which for those of you that don’t know is the founding document of our constitution, we the people have the right to enter into lawful rebellion if we feel we are being governed unfairly. Contrary to common belief our sovereign, the King, and his government are only there to govern us and do not rule us, and this must be done within the constraints of our common law, and the freedom asserted to us by such law. Nothing can become law in this country if it falls outside this simple construct, and article sixty-one shows quite clearly who really holds the power in this country, that is quite simply us the people; we have sovereignty, not any parliament, and nor can this be taken from us by any parliament who claim to have taken the peoples sovereignty."

With this a huge cheer came from most of the crowd. I glanced around and saw a lot of confused faces, which is always the case when people are presented with new information. I glanced back at the policy enforcement officers and they were looking a bit confused too. Sarah continued "The invocation of article sixty-one, the security clause of the magna carta as it's known, happened on the twenty third of march, two thousand and one, and was reported in the daily telegraph on the twenty fourth of march two thousand and one. There is also evidence of letters available on the internet between Robin Janvrin and the committee of the barons at the time. This means that I, along with all the peoples of this realm have a lawful duty under common law and constitutional law, to stand by the invocation of Article sixty-one, and whilst remaining loyal and lawful sovereign men and women, we have the right to enter into lawful rebellion." Sarah stopped and took a mouthful of water from a bottle she was holding.

"Since March the twenty third, two thousand and one, the crown has been disposed of all authority until we the people find redress and restore our common law and constitution. So, since the twenty third of march, two thousand and one we have had no lawful government, there are no courts of law with any authority at this time. We have been deceived by criminals and traitors in parliament. The government has been stripping away our rights and has invoked war on its own people. According to law, every man and woman has a legal and moral obligation to stand together under the security clause once it has been invoked, in order to preserve our constitutional rights. It is also every man and woman's job to inform and compel others to do the same, once having been made aware, and that would be common law in effect today. Put simply, that means standing our ground and living our freedom under law to defend our birthright, is the spirit of the law now." Sarah raised her right fist as she said the last few words then the roar that came up from the crowd was deafening. There were still some confused faces in the crowd, but most people understood Sarah's words, the noise died down and she continued.

"I want you all to remember my words today, I want you all to go away and research what I have said. We have no legitimate government at the moment, and we have no courts of law." the crowd applauded louder than ever. The people were slowly but surely waking up. The applause and cheers slowed down, and Sarah spoke again. "We have been deceived, not just since the twenty third of march two thousand and one, but for years and years before. What used to be a government with the interests of the people at heart has been hijacked by criminals, in love with money and power. Our courts are not here for justice, they are here for profit, our healthcare should be called sick care, and our education system is an indoctrination system. You will not have been taught this in school, but we have a bill of rights, and we have a constitution in the magna carta. We are deliberately not taught our rights in school because it's easier to take them away if we don't know we have them. I want you to study your rights and teach your children. I want you to learn to deal with the fake authority without fear. We must take back our rights and freedoms and never let them go again."

The roar from the crowd echoed around the square. The applause carried on for well over a minute, and only died down when Sarah motioned with her hands for silence, then Sarah continued "You as men and women are under no lawful obligation to obey the statutes, acts and mandates of this treasonous government. Their laws, which are actually only rules of a society, require the consent of the governed, and that is the individual consent, not the collective consent. You as men and women have the right to say no to their rules and regulations. They are men and women just like us, the only power they have is the power they have given themselves, or the power you grant them over you. Think about it, where does this power come from? One or two men and women have convinced other men and women that they have the right to tell you what you can and can't do. If there is no victim, then there is no crime. A man or woman has only committed a crime if there is a victim to make a claim. If you are a decent man or woman just going about your daily life and not hurting anyone, then why should you be bound by the rules of a bunch of hypocritical parasites, I mean these people even vote to give their selves a pay rise every year." There was laughter from the crowd, and it was clear that the people were listening, and Sarah was really wooing them, she continued.

"I am forty-six years old, and if you said that I have been aware of politics and politicians since I was ten, then that's thirty-six years, and in all that time I can honestly say, they have done nothing to change this country or the world for the better. They argue, fight and blame each other for the mess they have created. They lie, cheat and deceive us, they orchestrate wars to make money, they set agendas to relieve us of our freedoms and the money we break our backs to earn, then award each other with knighthoods and huge pay rises, not to mention the gold-plated pensions they give themselves." The crowd laughed again. I glanced back and saw some of the coppers joining in. Sarah addressed the police "Can I ask the police constables if they would look at the evidence of the treason that is taking place, and make a case against the politicians and the judges?" The crowd turned towards the policy enforcement officers, but not one of them wanted to step up and look at the evidence, not one of them even moved. Their lack of action spoke volumes, Truth, honesty and justice were way down the list.

"No takers?" Sarah said. "I thought not, so let me address you constables. You took an oath to the King, to uphold the common laws of this land, and to cause the peace to be kept, when you are doing this, you are acting lawfully as a police constable, and you have powers. When you are forcing the rules of the government, which does business as, and is registered as a corporation with company's house, then you are forcing company policy onto men and women, but the men and women have a right to say no thankyou Mr. policy enforcement officer, I don't want to obey company policy if it's not law, but you have not been taught this have you? How about I educate you and show you what these criminals have got you doing. How about we have a meeting and discuss the acts of treason and the unlawful administration courts, how about we discuss the truth for a change."

Sarah's words echoed through the now silent square. Some of the police were looking down at the ground, too ashamed to look the people in the eye and others just stared ahead with confused looks on their faces. Sarah spoke again.

"Who will give you the order to attack us today, when all we are doing is speaking the truth? Who tells you we are the enemy? Think about who's bidding you are doing, because there is an agenda behind this, and hitting us with batons or spraying us with chemicals is an act of aggression, it's not, and never can be peacekeeping. We as men and women have the right to defend ourselves, and the right to defend each other from tyranny. If that order comes today, will you bear arms against us, or will you question the motives of the order giver? You need to look deeper constables. At what point did you change from the friendly Bobby on the beat, catching criminals and doing good deeds, into the bullying paramilitary force you are becoming now? My time is up for today, but we have more information that you need to see so please take a leaflet from the men and women who are handing them out, and please research what I have spoken about today, it's important for our future and the futures of our children and grandchildren. Thank you for listening, best wishes." A long and respectful round of applause from every man and women in the audience finished Sarah's talk off.

The music started playing from the large speakers on the makeshift stage and almost immediately there was a bit of a commotion at the back of the crowd, I couldn't see clearly what was happening, but people were being pushed and shoved by the policy enforcement officers. The people weren't fighting back they were just trying to get out of the way. I moved toward the commotion to get a better view and could now see clearly what was happening, the police were targeting the leaflet distributors. They were snatching the leaflets from their hands and pulling at the bags they were carrying. One of the cowards pushed a young lady so hard that she fell and cracked her head heavily on the slabbed floor, a man who appeared to be with her, hit the tyrant square on the jaw and he dropped like the sack of shit that he was. Kicks and punches rained down on him from every direction as he was surrounded by a very angry mob. I could see blood pouring from the copper's face and head. Someone shouted "Enough, enough." And the mob stepped back and vanished into the crowd. The copper was trying to get back up but was collapsing and stumbling. Two of his colleagues ran to his aid and dragged him back through the crowd. The young lady was by the stage getting patched up by the first aiders, her male friend who knocked the copper out was by her side, he hadn't hesitated for a second to defend her from this unlawful attack and didn't leave her. I moved closer to the stage, ready to defend the couple if another attack was launched. The music volume was lowered, and Sarah took to the stage again "Ladies and gentlemen, please stay calm.

We are here to peacefully exchange information." Sarah motioned towards the young lady who was injured by the copper. "Would you come up on the stage please," the young lady didn't hesitate, she climbed the five steps onto the stage. Everyone could see her blood-soaked hair and clothes, and although she had been patched up temporarily, the bandage on her head was starting to soak through with blood.

Sarah addressed the crowd. "This young lady has committed no crime, she has not caused harm, loss or defrauded any man or woman here today, she is however a victim of a vicious assault; Would a member of the West Mainland police please arrest the policy enforcement officer who assaulted this lady?" Almost in unison the whole crowd turned and faced the police, many of whom had put their riot helmets on and were brandishing batons. "Is there a superior officer here who can arrest the man responsible.?" Sarah tried again but got no response. "What you are witnessing here is the usual cover up, and one rule for me and another for thee. We have the policy enforcement officers number" Sarah held up a yellow strip with numbers on it, it must have been ripped off the shoulder of the copper in the affray only moments earlier. "Is there an officer willing to do his duty today and arrest this young lady's attacker, one of you must know who officer seven four five eight is, one of you must have the courage to do the right thing. No takers again?" Sarah was addressing the coppers directly, and the crowd stood silently facing the police.

"You took an oath to uphold the common law and keep the peace, now I am asking just one of you to find and arrest policy enforcement officer seven four five eight and bring him to justice" Sarah's words echoed through the now silent square. "You there, sergeant, I can see you are in charge of these men and women," A rather chubby man with sergeant stripes painted in yellow on his riot helmet had stepped forward but immediately turned his back on the crowd and started to address the boys in blue. I was too far away to hear his words but by the actions of the police officers I could tell he was barking orders. They all started fastening their helmets and raising their batons in the air. They surged forward assaulting and pushing the people nearest to them.

"We are a peaceful crowd, and we are not here for violence." Sarah shouted into the microphone but that wasn't going to stop them. We knew this would happen today at some point, and the preparations for this attack had been going on for weeks, the meetings in churches, the discrete sharing of information and the willingness of people to fight for their freedom was about to be realized.

This square had been chosen for a reason, two sides had the usual shops , restaurants and bars and another side was entirely took up with a huge and very ornate council building, the fourth side was the only real entrance and exit point which consisted of a pedestrianized strip about six meters across that ran between two nondescript buildings , one of these buildings had no exit points onto the square apart from a standard size fire escape but the building on the left of the pedestrianized strip had a roller shutter door which was slowly rising. Whilst the police had had been preoccupied with the speeches and assaulting the young lady, the nondescript building had been slowly filling up with men and women, ready to administer justice in the event of an attack by the police. The police had positioned themselves in the worst possible place, the only way back out of the square was through the pedestrian strip but they had moved forward and to the right of it making it easy for the men and women behind the roller door too kettle the police in and block the exit.

The coppers hadn't noticed the roller door slowly rising and as the order to attack came from the fat sergeant they moved aggressively forward. The first row or two of men and women took the brunt of the aggression from the coppers but as the police soon realized the men and women were here to fight back. The police were being grabbed one at a time and dragged towards the stage area to be dealt with. For every copper there was six or seven men or women on them. They were forcibly detained, mostly with their own handcuffs, and their helmets were removed.

Men and women were still flooding out of the roller shutter door and joining in the fight. Some of the police were struggling so their legs were bound with cable ties. Their radios and weapons were removed, and one shoulder number was taken off their coats, then each copper was photographed with the number being held near their face to make identification easier. Warrant cards were removed from inside pockets and placed in separate bags with the shoulder number. Every time a copper was subdued, and it was safe for the men and women to go back into the fight they did, and what started as six onto one copper soon became seven or eight onto one. We were taking a few casualties, mostly baton strikes and cs gas injuries but importantly not one copper was deliberately harmed, they were restrained but not harmed in any way.

A van full of reinforcements screeched to a halt just beyond the pedestrian entrance, but as fast as they pulled up, they were dragged from the van and pulled into the square where their numbers, weapons, radios and warrant cards were removed but without any major injuries. The noise was dying down now as every copper was restrained and processed. Suddenly a loud smack rand out to my left, a young-looking man had got a bit exited and kicked a copper in the face, he was immediately jumped on and cable tied up. A young lady administered first aid to the copper, he would be ok, just a fat lip and a mouth full of blood. There were a few shouts and threats coming from the embarrassed officers, but they soon realized the hopelessness of their situation.

Another police van screeched to a halt on the road just at the end of the pedestrian walkway, and as the coppers jumped out, they were immediately surrounded, some of them were wrestled to the ground as they became violent.

The speakers crackled into life, and this time a gentleman in his fifties who I didn't recognize started to speak. "To all the members of the West Mainland police force, you have been lawfully detained by the men and women that you have attacked. You are all under arrest for various crimes against the people. You will not be harmed in any way, and your identities have been recorded. You will be formally charged and processed in due course. Your weapons have been removed, and you have all been restrained to prevent any further violence or injuries. This was a peaceful gathering for the purpose of sharing information, we were not endangering anybody, and no crimes were being committed. You chose to attack us, and we chose to exorcise our right to defend ourselves, and each other. Had you been acting as police constables and standing under your oath of office then none of this would have happened, but you chose to act as policy enforcement officers, and use violence against innocent men and women. You chose to force company policy onto us today. Your oath of office was and still is, to the King. You swore to uphold the common laws of the land, you did not swear to uphold the rules of this treasonous, corporate oligarchy. We have the right to convene a common law court, and we have the means in place to try every one of you. The men and women here today have had enough of being forced to obey the rules of this self-serving government, and we are sick and tired of being attacked by you and your colleagues."

The crowd remained respectfully quiet whilst then man spoke. "The excuse that you are just following orders will not wash, it didn't work for the Nazis at Nuremburg, and it won't work now. I suggest you all have a little think about your actions and when you realize that we outnumber you everywhere not just here in this square, maybe you will think twice about using violence against us. You are relatively small in number compared to your victims, and your victims have had just about enough. Now because we are good people, we haven't hurt you today, but if you continue to follow the orders and do the bidding of the criminals in government we will fight back, and you will lose. Ladies and gentlemen, I think it's time we left." And with that the microphone went quiet and the man exited the stage.

A huge round of applause went up from the crowd, and true to our word not one copper was harmed in any way apart from the earlier little kick in the chops that the over exited kid had administered to the handcuffed copper, and the cunt who hurt the leaflet lady who got exactly what he deserved. We all moved away as quickly as was safely possible without any pushing or shoving. I glanced back at the scene in the square, there must have been a hundred coppers, all sat down either hand cuffed, or cable tied, slowly trying to regain their composure. A large pile of weapons was piled up off to one side, and the only people who weren't coppers were the food vendors and two lads who were packing the stage and sound equipment away. They ignored the copper's pleas for help and just carried on with their work.

I was one of the last people to exit the square, and I immediately cut through a department store with an exit on the other side of the building. I grabbed a bottle of water from the fridge near the till and asked for a bag as I paid. I quickly swapped my cap for the woolly hat I had bought earlier, ensuring to keep my face down to avoid the cameras. I removed my coat and stuffed it into the carrier bag and headed for the door. I took one of the free paper masks from a box near the door and quickly slipped it on. Hopefully if the CCTV operators were trying to track me this would disguise me. As I exited the store, I immediately flagged a black cab down. I jumped in and just said "Bloxton please mate", I would ask the driver to stop in a mile or so when he was on a bus route and give him double the fare, I'd jump on the bus for the rest of the way.

I was smiling to myself about the coppers getting arrested but cussing myself for not filming it on the GoPro, but never mind, plenty of people were filming so no doubt it would be online later. "Just here will do mate." I said to the taxi driver. He protested in broken English, something about Bloxton and money, so I just gave him twenty pounds and said, "Keep the change." I exited the taxi and walked about forty yards to the nearest bus stop. I was on the main road to the town where I live so it didn't matter which bus came along as they all headed for the terminus.

The bus appeared just down the road, so I slipped the mask back on just before the bus came to a stop, with a couple of loud hisses the step lowered, and the doors opened. I got on the bus and paid the fare then went along the aisle to find a seat. I kept the mask on my face, and I had the wooly hat pulled down over my ears even though it wasn't very cold, but all these modern buses have CCTV cameras on them, and with how much we had dented the pride of the coppers, they would troll through every bit of footage to get revenge. The journey back was uneventful apart from the odd police van racing past.

As the bus pulled into the terminal, I could see several groups of police milling about and up to no good. I watched as they started to head towards the bus as we pulled in and came to a stop. Again, the doors hissed as they opened, and the steps lowered. I didn't rush to leave my seat and I let about ten people off before I even moved. A young lady was struggling with a pushchair and shopping bags, so I offered to help.

"Yes please." She chirped as I took a few bags towards the door for her.

I exited the bus and moved several meters away before stopping and helping the young lady rearrange the bags on the pushchair.

"Thank you." She said again.

"No problem." I replied. She had saved me from getting harassed as I left the bus, we must have looked like a couple as the policy enforcement officers had left me alone. I headed for the taxi rank and jumped in the cab at the front of the que, "Station Road, please mate." I said as I sat back in the seat. It's not where I lived but it was about two streets away, so only a minute's walk. The taxi pulled up and I paid the driver, again saying "Keep the change mate." The taxi pulled off leaving a plume of diesel smoke. I headed in the direction of home, removing the mask and taking a deep breath as I walked.

The key turned in the lock and I pushed the door open; the familiar smell of home filled my nostrils. With a turn of the night latch, I locked the door behind me. I shouted "Hello" as I passed the bottom of the stairs and a muffled "Alright dad." Came from my son who was in his room. I opened the fridge and poured myself a glass of orange juice before unlocking the back door and heading out into the garden to enjoy the rest of the afternoon's sunshine.

I sat down in the comfy swing chair, orange juice next to me, and smiled to myself. What a day, we had been building up to today for months, since the corporate government had unlawfully imposed movement restrictions, information restrictions, medical restrictions and a load more restrictions. Finally, the people are waking up and doing something about this nonsense.

My lad suddenly appeared around the corner of the shed and handed me the mobile phone. He had done exactly as I had asked him and made a few phone calls and sent out a few pre-scripted texts to some friends of mine. The phone records would show that I hadn't left the house all morning. "Cheers son." I said as he handed me the phone.

"Mark has called, but I told him you were asleep" my son replied.

"Good man, I will sort us some food out a bit later" I replied.

My lad headed off back to his computer and I started to scroll through the phone. I checked the responses my lad had text back to my friends to make sure nothing was left open ended then pressed on marks number in the phone. The phone rang about four times then Mark answered.

"How you doing kidda?" he asked in his familiar way.

"Fair too middling mate. How about you?"

"Not so bad thanks." Came marks reply.

"What are you and the lad up to later mate? me and the missus are having a bit of a celebration barbeque if you're up for it?"

"Sounds good mate, but I can't guarantee my lad will come, what time are you starting?" I asked.

"About half five, just bring a few beers, everything else is here." Mark replied.

"No probs mate, I'll see you later." I responded.

"See you later mate.", and with that the phone went dead.

I glanced at the phone screen and looked at the time, it was half past three. I took a sip of orange juice and put my head back onto the cushioned seat, I sat smiling to myself thinking about how the police would explain about being cable tied and arrested. The man who spoke last at the gathering earlier would serve papers onto all the policy enforcement officers. We gathered their names, numbers and warrant cards, despite this and all the evidence that would be presented to the courts, I bet not a single prosecution would ever come of it, as usual it would all just be denied and hidden but the people who were there and the millions who will watch the videos will know the truth.

9

"The truth will set you free, but it will piss you off first."

I took a last swig of my orange juice then headed inside to get ready for the barbeque. I stood in the shower for a good twenty minutes. Imagining the water washing the troubles of the past couple of years away. This is a little ritual I have, and it normally leaves me feeling upbeat and refreshed, and today was no exception. I exited the shower and dried myself with the large towel that is draped across the side of the bath, I wrapped the now damp towel around my waist and headed for the bedroom to put on some going out clothes, something I hadn't done for a long time. I retrieved my brown leather boots from their place in the wardrobe, I shouted along the landing to my son telling him to "Get ready" and got a muffled "Okay dad." In response. I polished my boots in the kitchen then headed back upstairs into the bathroom. A quick squirt of aftershave and I was good to go. I played my lad up about his spikey, gelled hair and in response he said, “At least I have some Baldy.” Whilst slapping the top of my head Benny Hill style.

We exited the house, and both realized immediately that our summer coats wouldn’t be warm enough, so we headed back in and changed jackets. I popped my new woolly hat on to keep the cold off my head. Neither of us had our mobile phones with us, as usual they don’t leave the house with us unless it’s for work or school. We had no government ID and by that, I mean anything linking us to a legal fiction, like a bank card or driver’s license. We headed down to the high street and into the off license to buy some beers for me and some pop for my lad. I grabbed an expensive bottle of wine for our hosts then exchanged a few pleasantries with the lad behind the counter as I paid, and he bagged our purchases up.

Now the movement restrictions haven't really been lifted for us unvaccinated but considering events that happened today I didn't care one bit. With every new bit of information, I was getting regarding the actual rights of the policy enforcement officers and the corrupt administrative courts I was confident that there was not a lot they could really do if we all just said, "Not today thank you." And maintained our position as private men and women, not getting tricked into giving a legal name and becoming a fictional character in their little game.

The walk to Marks is about a mile, and the route we are taking should keep us away from any policy enforcement patrols, but just in case, I had briefed my lad on what to do again. If the shit hit the fan, I would take on the coppers and he was to run to my sisters, but hopefully it wouldn't come to that.

As it happened, we had a lovely early autumn evening walk, with no interference from anyone. We chatted about school and what my lad wanted to do with his life. It was just like old times, and it felt nice.

Before long we were walking up the familiar driveway to Marks house, and I could already smell the barbeque. I rang the doorbell and after a short while Mark appeared, opening the door revealing a spatula in one hand and a beer in the other. He immediately made a fuss of my lad, shaking him firmly by the hand and commenting on how much he had grown. My lad's attention was immediately distracted by Marks teenage daughter, who he secretly had a crush on. Me a Mark warned them both to be good and we got the usual, "Shut up." and "Get lost." as a response from them simultaneously. The two kids disappeared into the lounge to play computer games with the other youngsters who were there.

"Quite a result today wasn't it kidda?" Mark said as we made our way through the warm kitchen and out into the garden, where Mark had a canopied area for these events.

"A real result Mark. Every one of them was placed under citizen's arrest and handcuffed or cable tied. One dickhead booted a copper in the face, but we cable tied him and left him for them to deal with." I replied enthusiastically.

"I am going to introduce you to a couple of people who are on our side so to speak but be a bit guarded with details of your activities from today as I am only just getting to know the one couple, they are friends of the wife." Mark half whispered towards me as we crossed the patio area.

I had already met a couple of people at the get-together, and it would be good to catch up with them. Mark introduced me to the new couple,

"This is MR DAVID RICHARDS and his wife MRS EMILY RICHARDS." I knew from marks formal introduction and his use of their legal fiction names that this was the couple

I should be cautious around. He introduced me as Dan, which gave nothing away.

I immediately said, “Don’t be so formal Mark, David and Emily, it’s nice to meet you both.” As I shook David by the hand. We exchanged a few pleasantries then I excused myself to grab a beer and a burger. Another old friend called Allen shook me firmly by the hand, we laid bricks together years ago and both our hands were like leather.

“How you doing lad?” came Allen’s familiar greeting,

“Not so bad olden.” I replied with half a mouth full of burger.

“Good job in the city today, I bet the atmosphere was electric?” Alan said, a little louder than I liked. I raised my finger to my lips, indicating to him to keep the conversation a little quieter. He just winked at me and smiled.

“It was awesome Al, they never knew what was going on, we had about three or four times the number of men and women they were expecting, and the warehouse was full mate. The look on their faces when we were arresting them was priceless, and best of all there was only a couple of injuries, one when a young lad got over exited and booted a copper and one cunt got what he deserved for flooring a young lady." I replied, filling Alan in on a few details. I occasionally checked over my shoulder to see who was listening. MR and MRS RICHARDS were out of earshot, so I gave the full account of the event to Alan, from the copper on the bus journey to the hasty change of clothes in the department store. This was a war that we the people were winning.

Several beers, three burgers and two hours later, the barbeque was in full swing, and the combination of cold autumn air and alcohol was loosening everyone up. It was time to try and get to know MR and MRS RICHARDS and see what their opinion of this nonsense was.

"MR RICHARDS." I said extending my hand out as I spoke.

"Please call me David," He replied shaking my hand firmly. "And this is my wife, Emily." he said as he motioned towards his rather drunk wife with his hand.

"Emily how are you? I'm Dan." I said as I introduced myself.

"Slightly tipsy Dan, that's how I am as it's my first night out in two bloody years, thanks to this poxy government and their bullshit." Came her drunken reply. I liked Emily Richards already.

"I do apologies for my wife; she doesn't get out much." David said with a laugh. Emily extended her middle finger in David's direction.

"Nice to meet you, Dan." Emily said as she walked away. I raised my drink slightly and nodded in her direction with a smile on my face.

"It's nice to meet people with a similar opinion of our government." I said to start the conversation.

"I think they are a bunch of cunts, pardon the expression." David replied.

"Cunts are useful David; these people are criminals." I responded, trying to push for a little more info.

"My thoughts exactly Dan. Do you know we got stopped by some jumped up little prick in a uniform on the way over here, he started spouting off a load of nonsense statutes and rules that he said I had to obey?" David said rather animatedly. I could see that he was reliving the encounter in his head, and the alcohol was helping enhance the memory of the interaction more.

"What was your response to him?" I asked, trying to pry a bit more and sus David out.

"I wanted to say get fucked piglet, but I asked if he was there on his oath, then I asked if I had committed a crime and when he said, "No sir you haven't committed a crime." I said, "Am I free to go?" He didn't even speak to me Dan; He just waived me off with his hand. Me and the wife just walked off, without looking back." David said with a pleased look on his face.

"Fair play David, but I don't understand how you did that? Why didn't he arrest you?" I asked, trying to play dumb.

"You don't have to do business with them Dan, as long as you don't contract with them or refuse, then you are the master, and they are the servant. Answer a question with a question;" David exclaimed. Of course, I knew all this already, but I wanted to find out what David knew and if he had anything new to offer.

"Explain it to me again Dave?" I questioned.

"When the copper comes up to you and asks you for your name, he is trying to get what they call joinder, if you give your legal name, example MR DAVID RICHARDS, then this gives him power over you as you have basically contracted with him, but if when he asks you for your name you answer him with the question, like "Am I obliged to give you a name?" his response should be "No you're not obliged." You see Dan, everything with them is contract. They are basically asking you if you want to do business with them. They are nothing more than a private security business touting for work. If I'm walking down the street minding my own business and I am stopped then why should I agree to a contract with them. It's a scam Dan, all of it is a scam, they are just men and women who have convinced themselves that they have authority over you. By giving the legal name, you are considered to be a thief because that name is not yours to use. Imagine it's like an overcoat, when you slip the MR DAVID RICHARDS overcoat on, you become liable for this fictional entity. They can't do business with you as a man or woman, so they trick you into being this fiction. They have rules for everything Dan, and there's always a monetary value for breaking their rules, in reality they have made everything a sin and then monetized that sin. One or two men and women sitting back and living the life of riley, raking in the cash because you did something that they made a rule up for. Do you know that we have a Bill of Rights in this country?" David stopped for a breath and let me answer, he was in full flow now,

"No Dave I didn't. "I replied with a slightly confused look on my face.

"Well, we have a Bill of Rights published in 1689, it sets out certain civil rights that we have, part of it says, only a judge can fine you in a court of law and that is after a trial by jury. But they repealed that law so any tom, dick or harry can bloody fine you, answer me this, why are profit making organizations, like police forces and councils getting away with fining men and women for non-criminal offenses? I'll tell you why it's because we willingly contract with them by wearing the legal fiction overcoat. If you get a parking fine issued by the local council, it is an offer to contract, the paperwork is an invoice, it all looks very official and there's lots of "if's" and "you may be's" written on it, but when you look deeper, they are just tricking you into paying. You don't have to contract with them Dan. They use unlawful administrative courts, finding people guilty of these imaginary crimes without any due process, they have whole warehouses of machines printing these fines off day and night twenty-four hours a day, seven days a week and three hundred and sixty-five days a year. Not one of these cases has been Infront of a judge and not one of the fines is lawful, but it's our ignorance that is letting them get away with it. When you question their system, they just ridicule, threaten or make up another rule to reinforce the rule that you have questioned." David stopped talking and took several mouthfuls of his beer.

"So, stopping us and asking for our carbon output figures or requesting our identification is unlawful then?" I asked.

"It's not unlawful for them to ask but you are under no lawful obligation to reply, you have the right to remain silent so as not to incriminate yourself, this includes not giving a name or helping the policy enforcement officer in any way. He or she cannot force you to do anything at all if you haven't committed a crime. There isn't a man or woman alive who has the right to force you to do anything, but when we start giving men and women legal titles then convincing other men and women that they will be in big trouble if they don't join in the game that they are playing, we start to get problems. Yes, we need laws to protect victims of crime, but the real criminals are making rules up to line their pockets or further their own agendas. Look at the climate change agenda now, they are spraying tones of shit into the sky's every day from the airplanes, bouncing frequencies off the chemical trails that the planes pump out and then blaming us driving the kids to school in a diesel car for the problem they have created." David paused for a breath then sighed deeply.

"They want us all driving electric cars Dan, electric cars that have so much technology in them that they can track every movement that you make, they can remotely control these devices and turn them off if they don't like you doing something or saying something. The construction of a battery powered car is much dirtier and worse for the planet than the construction of a petrol or diesel car. Young children are mining the minerals that go into the batteries on the cars but guess what they don't mention that bit. I would like to make a little bet with you Dan, and that is if we could look at who stands to make the most money and have the most control over us from the climate agenda then it will be the very same people who are creating the problem in the first place. Problem, reaction and solution. They create the problem to get a reaction from you then sell you the solution and make a tidy profit from it." David took a long swig of his beer whilst I nodded politely. He was in full swing now, so I let him continue.

" They have just convinced us all that we are going to die from a virus so they can sell billions of vaccines and tons of medical equipment at huge profits to themselves and their mates, and when the virus loses credibility they move on and start a war to sell weapons then they spray the skies to sell salvation from the weather, oh as long as you give them nearly every penny that you earn you will be safe. If they were that concerned about the planet and climate change then they would stop all forms of pollution tomorrow, what they want is to scare you into giving them the energy you have gained in the form of money" David stopped his speech, he had been in full flow and a small audience had been listening to his talk. He had simplified the conversation for me to understand but this was information I knew well.

"I overstand you David" I broke the silence. David looked surprised at my use of the word overstand. I didn't understand or stand under his words. I overstood his words, meaning not only did I comprehend what he had said but I fully recognized why he had said it.

I questioned David a bit more "Why do we have to do business with these corporations David?"

David took a deep breath before continuing. "When our parents are forced to register our birth,"

"What do you mean by forced? My parents weren't forced to register me, were they?" I responded slightly feigning my shock at his statement.

David continued "Your parents would of received a letter and somewhere on that polite letter asking them to come and register little Dans happy birth, there would have been a section that said if you don't register little Dans birth then you will have to give us some money, so yes Dan I think they were forced and when you combine this with the indoctrination they would have received at school then they were not only forced but tricked into doing it, but any way back to the original question, by registering your live birth at the registry office they unwittingly created a legal fiction this legal fiction is you Dan, well not you the little boy or living man but a corporation that sounds just like your name and from that moment on you have been tricked into believing that you are this corporation. When you went to school in the mornings the teacher shouted out the name of the corporation and you were taught to say "Yes Miss or here Miss." When a letter comes to your house it is addressed to the corporation MR DAN, whatever your Sir name is, it's written in all block capital letters and in black ink. Tombstones are written in block capitals as it's the writing of the dead Dan, they have tricked you into being, and answering for this dead legal fictionally created piece of paper so they can make you join in the game and do business with other dead legal fiction entities. A living man or woman can't do business with a corporation because the corporation is not a living being, you can't take it for a beer or have dinner with it but when they lower your status from a man to a corporate fiction then they have you." David continued as he had a captive audience.

"We are taught from an early age that we must get permission to do this and a license to do that, it's all bullshit Dan, they take away your right to do something and sell it back to you in the form of a license. A license is permission to do something on or with someone else's property, well do they own the right to drive, do they own the roads. You must pay them a percentage for everything you do, or get their permission, well who the fuck put them in charge?" David was getting angry as he spoke, I was really starting to warm to him now.

"How does voting work, I mean why don't they just tell us who is in charge instead of asking us to pick?" I asked as innocently as I could.

"When you vote you are just picking the new CEO of the corporation Dan, I mean you are voting for the left wing or the right wing, but the wings are attached to the same bird. By registering to vote you are consenting to be governed, and by putting a little cross in that box you are saying you can't write your name and you are illiterate, and you are treated as a child that needs to be looked after. Do you really think they would be so stupid as to let us choose who we really wanted in charge? We don't get to select the candidates, Dan; they tell us who the candidates are. Your vote as you call it, is just used to gauge public opinion." David paused and took a long drink from his glass.

"Back to the courts being a business or a corporation, why can't you just say, "No thank you, I don't want to do business with you." I mean I don't have to buy stuff from a shop or eat in a particular restaurant if I don't want to, so why am I forced to go to court?" I asked, prying more from David.

"Because you are tricked into believing you are the legal fiction name Dan. You are not taken to court; you willingly go there because you have been invited to represent the fiction. When you go to court you have to stand up as the judge enters the court, you stand under his authority, he asks your name you give the legal name and confirm that you are the corporate fiction, then through sleight of hand they make you the man, into a fictional character that can play in their fictional courts. Games are played on courts. They don't care about right or wrong, they care about the profits they can make. Living men and women can't be heard in court that's why you employ someone to represent you, they are re-presenting themselves as you or speaking for you, a solicitor or lawyers first duty is to the court and its not to you, it's better not to go to their mickey mouse administrative court." David took a breath, so I asked another question.

"I thought it was only the traffic courts that were administrative, I mean surely a court with a judge or magistrate isn't administrative?"

David took a deep breath before answering "Unfortunately not Dan, any court where the magistrate or judge can decide the outcome is administrative, and as you know there's no jury in a magistrate court and a judge can instruct the jury in other courts, another thing they don't tell you is the true roll of the jury. The jury is not only there to decide if you are guilty of committing a crime based on the evidence, but they are there to decide whether the law is a just law, and not just nonsense. This is another reason they are trying to stop your right to trial by jury Dan. Juist imagine how much money they would lose if everyone demanded a trial by jury, then the jury found everyone not guilty because the law was nonsense in the first place. Do you know there are no real courts of law in this country at the moment. There isn't even a lawful government since article sixty-one was invoked back in 2001." David paused for another sip of his beer.

"Explain that again David, the bit about the jury." I asked, finally learning something new.

"What they don't want you to know is that the jury's job is not only to decide whether the man or woman on trial is guilty, but it's also to decide whether the law that put them there is really a law. By that I mean it they make up a rule that men called john can't eat eggs on a Sunday, but a man called john is caught eating eggs on a Sunday, and he is daft enough to put himself willingly before the court, then the true role of the judge is to convene the court and the job of the jury is to decide whether john is in fact guilty but also whether the nonsense that put him there is in fact a just law, now apply that to most of the bollocks we are fined for and you will see why they are trying to stop our right to trial by jury, because the jury could nullify their bullshit rules. It's called jury nullification." David sighed as he stopped speaking.

"Back to the government corporation thing David. If they make the laws and they are really a private company, so to speak, then why do we have to obey them?" I asked.

"If the truth were known Dan, then we would have to individually consent to the fake laws, by that I mean the statutes, acts and mandates of these criminals. Things made up by these parasites are not laws, they are no more than rules of a society, and these rules require the consent of the governed, and that is the individual consent not the collective consent. Individually as men and women we should be able to say yes or no to their rules, it's called consent, but they don't really want you to know that." David's replies were coming thick and fast, so I carried on.

"So, I have the right to withdraw my consent?" I asked.

"Yes of course, we all do but we don't know how to do it. We are all indoctrinated at school, taught to obey authority, when in reality there is no authority. If me and you were born on the same day, at precisely the same second, and we both grow alongside each other as equals then one day you go off and join the police, at what point do you suddenly get this imaginary authority over me, because if you believe that saying an oath, which is just manmade words, Infront of someone else who got their power by saying a man-made oath, then you are mistaken. It's like government, the only power government has over us is the power we give them. Yes, we need the government to organize some stuff and set things up to make the country run, which is what we pay them for but what we don't need is a fictitious entity ruling our lives. The people making up these rules remain anonymous by hiding behind "The government" they make up rules that help their friends and family out and remove rights from me and you. We are the ones with the real power Dan, it's us that should be calling the shots. They should do as we tell them and not just do what they want." David's words were flowing now he had a captive audience.

David continued "We are scammed every day by men and women who hide behind their fake authority. They are lining their own pockets and the pockets of their friends. Take for instance local councils. They have no authority over you, but they issue fines for parking, fines for silly red lines on the road they have zones for this and zones for that, emissions zones, bus lanes and all sorts of shit they can fine or charge you for, but in reality, they are the paid caretakers of the local area and not the owners of the area or the roads. If you drive into the city, you must pay an emissions charge if you go into certain areas, what the fuck are people doing paying it? The so-called local authority has sold the right to charge people for travelling through land they don't own, they have sold the right to charge this shit to a private company, no doubt owned by one of their mates or a family member of someone high up. They have just stuck some cameras up and a load of signs and said go ahead make as much money as you can scamming any fool who pays it. We own the roads because it's us who pays to build them. The best of it is that you have no contract with these private companies, so let them send you a fine and when it comes return it with "no contract" written across it in red ink. Don't even open it and don't accept it. Learn how to do return to sender. It's not addressed to you anyway; it's addressed to your legal fiction. Better still throw it in the bin, don't give any life to the fiction, by responding you agree to be the fictional character who the letter is addressed to. If none of us contracted, they would be out of business. One or two men and women have got very rich off these scams, it's all made to look very official, photographs of your car and if you pay now without asking any questions then we will only unlawfully fine you £35 instead of unlawfully fining you £70, it's all a scam. It's an offer to contract and people fall for it because they have been tricked into believing they have broken a law, well they haven't as long as there is no victim then there is no crime, it's the same as the copper asking your name, he's trying to contract with you." David stopped for a good gulp of his drink.

"How did we all end up so dumbed down David?" I asked for the benefit of the others who were listening intently.

"Because they start tricking you as early as possible and then keep tricking you for the rest of your life. Nothing is as it appears and when you start to see through the bullshit it all becomes more transparent. Did you know we have a Bill of Rights in this country, we also have the Magna Carta, we have ways of getting redress or things put right, but it has been covered up, and the police and courts are so corrupt that it will take nothing short of a full-blown revolution to make things right."

“I heard there was something called section sixty-one of the Magna Carta, and some lords enacted it or something?” I asked playing dumb.

“Your close Dan, it is article sixty-one of the Magna Carta, and it was the barons who enacted it on the twenty third of march two thousand and one. Since that date we have had no lawful government” David repeated what I had heard earlier in the square.

“So why haven’t we heard about it on the news?” I pushed for more.

“Because every news outlet in the world, every newspaper, magazine, tv news channel and so on and so forth is owned by about six corporations and they control what we find out. It’s all a movie Dan, all of it. The government, courts, police and local authorities all rely on secrecy. They only let certain people know certain things, it’s a big club and we aren’t in it” David answered enthusiastically.

“Well, what can we do about it?” I asked as I raised my can of beer up to my lips.

“We can educate ourselves Dan and educate each other. Half of the police aren’t told what they are involved in. they truly believe the government has the right to dictate to us how we should live our lives, they truly believe you should be punished for breaking man-made rules. They believe they have the right to assault us on the orders of another man or woman, then if we fight back, they run and hide behind the courts to put us in jail. We as men and women have the right to defend ourselves regardless of who our attacker is, if we haven’t committed a crime then we have the right to defend ourselves, we must fight back, we need to remove our consent to be governed and policed by these corporate entities. Now is the time to fight back before any more of our rights are removed. We are under constant surveillance with the phones we carry, they track our every move, recording our conversations, constantly listening and tracking who we are with.

Pretty soon they will stop cash as money, they will monitor every transaction that we make, stealing not just the twenty percent of our wages that they really aren't entitled to but every penny that they want. Just imagine you go through a speed camera and they take the money before the bulb on the flash has even cooled down, you post an anti-government post on social media and they freeze your bank account or they pass a law saying they are entitled to fifty percent of your money each week because of climate change, how are you going to stop them Dan, we need to say no before it's too late. Do you know there are fucking idiots in some countries having microchips implanted in their hands so they can open doors in the factories they work in, or get drinks in the canteen by scanning their hands, look how easy it is to pay for stuff just by touching a card against a machine. Why can't people see where this is leading, vaccine passports are just the start of it.

They sell it as more freedom but in reality, its enslavement." David stopped for a breath.

"People are fighting back David, only today some people were at a peaceful rally in the city, when they were attacked by violent criminals disguised as police constables. The people made citizens arrests on these men and women as no man or woman has the right to use weapons against non-violent human beings unless it's in self-defense. When they choose to use a weapon if you haven't committed a crime then they become the aggressor and you become the victim. If they are forcing company policy onto you, which is basically any fake law that the fictitious entity calling itself government, has created with the fake power it has given itself, they you have the right to remove your consent without fear of punishment." I said with conviction.

"But how do we stand up to the corruption and the deceit?" David asked with a hint of despair in his voice.

“We must stand together David, every man, woman and child. It’s no good that only a handful of us have this knowledge. We need to educate everyone about how to deal with these criminals.” I answered David again and he began to see that I knew a bit more than I was letting on.

“Please excuse me for a bit.” I said as I took the last mouthful of my beer.

“No problem, Dan I’ll catch up with you later.” David replied as he raised his drink in my direction, I nodded and smiled as I started to walk away towards the house. I headed inside to use the downstairs toilet.

After using the toilet, I went to find my lad. I popped my head around the lounge door and saw all the kids having a right old-time playing computer games on the large tele. I nodded at my lad, and he put his thumb up to signal that he was ok. I winked back at him then retreated to the kitchen to grab another beer. Mark was standing in the kitchen smiling from ear to ear whilst chatting with a friend of his, no doubt the beer was adding to the daft look on his face. It was nice to be finally having a night out and a few beers with friends even though it wasn't officially allowed, but fuck them, no victim no crime, and reports of government parties during lock down were being leaked onto the news, so what's good for the goose is good for the gander.

I grabbed another cold can of beer from the fridge and shut the door, nodding at Mark as I made my way back outside into the cool and now less smokey air.

"Dan" David called me and gestured for me to join him. "How did you know about what happened in the city today?" David asked.

"Oh, a friend of mine was shopping there and was nearly caught up in it. She said some people stood up to the policy enforcement officers and it looked like they arrested them." I lied convincingly; I wasn't going to give too much away as I hadn't quite sussed David out yet.

"Oh, I just thought you may have been there from how you spoke." David replied trying to find a crack in my story.

"No but I had a good account of what went on." I replied cautiously.

"Are we allowed to arrest the police Dan?" David asked, fishing for a little more information.

"Of course, David, if they are not standing under their oath as police constables, that is if they are not upholding the common law but instead choose to force the statute law onto nonconsenting men and women, then we not only have the right, but also a moral duty to arrest them and get them into a court to be dealt with for their crimes." I answered David's question.

"But the courts are as corrupt as the police." David rightly said.

"We the people have the right to convene a common law court, I know we wouldn't get justice in the unlawful administrative courts, but the common law court would provide the remedy we need." I answered David again.

"Is that possible, I mean don't you have to be a judge to hold court?" David responded, digging deeper still.

"No, we can appoint a judge ourselves, and as long as the correct procedure is followed, we may get justice." I replied.

The conversation was cut short as I heard a commotion coming from the house. I dropped my beer and ran inside; I was greeted by the sight of policy enforcement officers trying to push past Mark at the front door. I immediately headed out of the back door, shouting to David to back me up. We ran through the side gate to be greeted by about six or seven coppers. I put myself straight in between the door and the aggressive coppers.

"Move aside" The nearest copper shouted.

"Get off this property if you don't have a warrant from a lawful court. What is the nature of your business constable? You are here as a constable tonight, aren't you? Are you here on your oath tonight? Get back to the edge of the drive." I ordered.

"Move yourselves." Mark shouted next to me.

"We have reports," the copper started but I cut the copper off.

"Get back or you will be arrested for trespass;" I exclaimed. There were more of us than them, all the men and a few of the women from the party were on the drive now slowly moving the policy enforcement officers back. "Who is your duty inspector? Get him here now, tell him there has been a trespass and I am holding him accountable. Get back now" I ordered again. David was doing the same routine next to me, and I knew Mark would be demanding that the duty inspector attend the party.

We backed the coppers up to the edge of the drive and they retreated to the pavement. One copper drew his taser gun, I immediately moved in front of him and said, “You better kill me with the first shot sunshine, now put that weapon away.”

He pointed the gun straight at my chest. “Erm, I have the right.” He stammered as he spoke.

“You have no right to draw a weapon on another human being. Who gave you that right, who do you think you are?” I shouted in his face.

“Sir, if we could just,” a young lady copper interjected.

“I am not a sir, constable, I am man, nothing more or nothing less, you are men and women, nothing mor and nothing less, now stay back.” I ordered.

They moved back a few feet and left the young lady to do the talking. The other men had lined themselves up in front of the coppers, ready to deal with any unlawful attack. “If we could just ask whose house this is and take a few details then we can leave.” The female copper said.

“Are we obliged to give you any details constable? Are you acting as a police constable this evening or are you trying to force company policy onto us?” Mark questioned her.

“We have had reports of an illegal gathering at this address, and the current laws say we can fine the organizer ten thousand pounds. Who organized this party?” She tried again.

“Only a judge can fine you in a court of law, and that is after you have had a trial by jury constable, are you saying you are a judge tonight? Now think carefully about your answer as you are now on the record.” I replied to her demand. The ladies in our group were all filming on their phones as evidence of the unlawful intrusion.

“We have the right to take your details under the nineteen eighty-four pace acts.” She tried again.

“Let me stop you their constable, you have no right to force any statute, act or mandate of the treasonous government onto any man, woman or child without their individual consent. As a man standing here today, I have removed my consent to be governed, and therefore all government created, legislative laws are not applicable to me. Me and these men and women have not committed any crime, there is no victim here except us. You have barged onto this property uninvited, you have threatened us, and pointed weapons at us, I would like you to arrest each other for the crimes of common assault, trespass, breach of our peace and attempted robbery, and you young lady have tried to impersonate a judge so arrest each other, failure to do so will result in you being all being charged with dereliction of duty, now arrest each other." I demanded. They were looking at each other very confused, now we had stood our ground and didn't respond to any of their bullshit.

"Where is the duty inspector, I want him or her here now" Mark demanded.

“What is your name and number?” I asked the female pc.

“I’m not prepared,” she stammered but I cut in.

“Not prepared to give me your name and number.” I finished her sentence. “Name and numbers of all of you now.” I demanded.

“But” She went to protest again.

“Name and numbers now young lady, or I will arrest you for impersonating a police constable.” I raised my voice, not giving her a chance to think.

“But erm its two, zero, seven, five, PC Joanne Wells.” She stammered.

“Good now you.” I said, pointing at another one.

“Its three, one, eight, five PC Richard Pryor.” he said cautiously.

“And what nick are you from PC Pryor?” I demanded in a more authoritative tone.

"Bloxton." Came the short response. With this another car pulled up, and an older looking copper got out in a hurry. He headed straight for me and started to draw his batten. The metallic snap was loud as the sections of the telescopic weapon locked into place. He raised the batten above his head as he closed the distance between us. I shot my left arm up in the direction of the batten that was rapidly heading towards my shoulder, parrying it nicely down and locking his arm against my body, my right leg shot forward with the toes of my foot curled back, striking the copper in the shin, causing a little involuntary scream to leave his mouth. I quickly span him onto my hip, took his balance then unceremoniously dumped him on the floor, taking the wind out of him. I was all over him; my arm had slipped straight under his chin and the rear naked choke that I had him in was doing the job. He was frantically trying to pull my arm off his neck but then resorted to tapping my arm like it was some sort of submission competition. Mark and the other men had moved forward to protect me from any heroism from the younger coppers. I kept the choke on just until the point of unconsciousness then threw the copper away from me causing him to roll onto his side and gasp for air. I immediately grabbed his handcuffs from the belt around his waist and pulled his limp arms behind his back. The other coppers were frantically drawing their weapons but Mark, David and everyone else were already moving forward preventing them from getting at me. I clicked the handcuffs into place.

"Stop" I shouted as loudly as I could. Everyone froze and just stared at me. "I am arresting this man for assault with a deadly weapon, now I need you to assist me constable." I shouted in the direction of the female copper.

She stammered "Let him go" as she started to move forward.

"Stop" I shouted, "If you help to free him then you will be guilty of the crime of release."

The scene was funny, with nobody really knowing what to do. The lads on my side were more than ready for the scrap, the ladies were filming the evidence on their phones and the coppers were just staring at each other open mouthed. The female coppers eyes were bulging out her head on stalks and sergeant copper who I had handcuffed was now regaining his ability to talk. I broke the silence, "I have made a citizen's arrest on this man for assault with a deadly weapon and breaching my peace, I would like one of you to assist me in pressing charges."

"Mate just step back, and we will sort him out." One of the male coppers said as he cautiously stepped forward. I pushed myself up and backwards with the lads still protecting me.

The copper grabbed the sergeant's arm and helped him up. He was still winded from the heavy landing on the floor, and he limped slightly from the shin kick. As the copper escorted him to the police car, he looked over his shoulder and managed to say "Cunt" as he made eye contact with me. Still no arrest though.

"Sir, it seems that we have a little dilemma here" the copper said as he returned from the car.

"I'll repeat it for you again constable, I am not a Sir as I have no legal title. I am man, nothing more, nothing less." I cut in before he carried on.

"Okay mate, can we resolve this issue without anyone getting into trouble, I mean you did assault a police officer." He tried it on.

"On the contrary constable, the video evidence, and eyewitness accounts of the events this evening will show you lot trying to force statute law, and company policy onto nonconsenting men and women, then a man attacking me without warning and me using very reasonable force to defend myself, and restrain my attacker. You then failed to do your duty as I asked for assistance to arrest the criminal, but you all failed to help. You are all men and women, nothing more nothing less, you are acting in a fictional capacity as policy enforcement officers and trying to manufacture our consent to do business with you. You don't have the right to force the policies of a corporation on to other men and women, and that man in the back of the vehicle had no right to attack me." I stopped for a breath and waited for a comment from the coppers. "We, that is all of us here constable, are victims of deceit. You and your colleagues have been tricked into forcing company policy onto us, and we are victims of that policy. Now about tonight's events, the only crimes committed this evening were committed by you, and your colleagues. You trespassed on this peaceful gathering, you tried to force company policy onto us then one of you tried to assault me with a deadly weapon. You have failed to arrest my attacker and now you are bargaining with us. swearing a man-made oath to serve someone, doesn't give you the right to force company policy onto us. I think you need to take a little look at what the government has you doing before you all find yourselves in a real court of law."

"We are just doing our job mate." The female copper protested.

"That excuse didn't work at Nuremburg for the Nazis, and it won't work now princess. Now we have the evidence of what happened tonight, so if we have any trouble or reprisals then we will proceed against all of you, I suggest you all fuck off and leave us alone" I barked back at her. With that, and without another single word from the coppers, they got into their cars and left.

I immediately turned to mark and smiled from ear to ear "Come on son, let's get you a drink." Mark said, placing an arm around my shoulder as we turned to head back inside.

We headed back through the rear gate and into the garden, Mark appeared with a bottle of single malt whiskey and poured us all a good measure into some shot glasses, he tapped the side of his glass with a knife and announced in his posh voice, "I would like to propose a toast to the truth and justice." He raised his glass and we all repeated "To truth and justice." I gulped the golden-brown liquid down in one go and immediately grimaced as the whiskey burned my throat. Mark immediately topped my glass up and we all started to relax a little.

We knew there would be more harassment, but they probably wouldn't try it tonight. As the night wore on, I chatted more and more with David. His knowledge of the treason being committed by the government and how to deal with the policy enforcement officers was excellent. He explained article sixty-one in more depth and gave me several more avenues to explore.

All good things must come to an end and as the time approached midnight I went and found my lad and said, “Be ready in ten minutes son” I got the usual look of disappointment in return. I headed back outside and said “goodbye” to the hosts and went to find David, as I extended my hand in his direction he reached into his coat and pulled out a piece of paper, he shook me firmly by the hand and then held out the paper in my direction. “A gift for you and Mark, Dan. After watching you deal with the coppers tonight, I decided these would be of much more use to you and Mark than me and the missus.” I unfolded the piece of paper and read the words printed on it. I immediately called Mark over to join us and showed him the paper. “Thank you, David.” I said folding the paper back up and slipping it into my pocket.

David had given me and Mark two tickets to an event at the town hall for Monday night, an event where we could possibly spread some truth. The event is a popular televised show and just the place to ask the questions we wanted answered.

As we exited the front door Mark made a fuss of my lad then shook me firmly by the hand, “See you tomorrow night kidda.” Mark said as we walked down the drive. I nodded in reply and put my arm around my son’s shoulder only to be brushed off straight away. There was a slight chill in the air, and it was a nice clear night, we only had about a mile to walk, and we stuck to the side roads and the long walkway that skirted the park, hopefully we wouldn’t get any more harassment tonight but company policy at the moment seems to be to harass everyone.

10

"A child educated only at school is an uneducated child."

George Santayana

As we came to the end of the walkway, we went through the zig zag cycle gates and walked out onto the well-lit road that runs along the bottom of the park, the trees to the left of us were still in leaf and were rustling as there was a slight breeze. The houses to our right had lights on and the televisions could be seen flickering through the curtains of some of the windows. The streetlights were illuminating the whole road and making the trees glow with a tinge of yellow. A pair of headlights appeared at the bottom of the road, and I had a sinking feeling in my stomach. We could have quickly darted to our left into the park but with how well the road was lit, plus the headlights, we would have been seen.
"Remember plan A son, get to your aunties

if you need to." I said to my lad as the car drew ever nearer.

"Fuck em dad" came the blunt reply.

"We will discuss your language later son, but your right, fuck em." I replied with a smile.

The car was visible now and despite the headlights dazzling us we could clearly see it was the policy enforcement officers, probably up to no good. Hopefully they would see that we were just a father and son minding our own business and leave us alone.

The car stopped about three meters away from us and I could see there were only two coppers in there. The passenger side window was going down and a face came into view as we drew alongside the car.

"Evening sir." Came the first attempt to engage us.

"Are you implying I have legal title constable." I responded.

"I don't know what you mean Sir." He tried again.

"Keep walking Son." I said to my lad The driver of the car put it in reverse and slowly kept up with us as we walked away.

"Do you mind stopping when I am talking to you Sir." The copper snarled.

"We are under no lawful obligation to do business with you or the corporation you work for. We are just two men walking home, minding our own business, now leave us alone." I responded politely but firmly.

The driver accelerated back at speed and stopped the car about twenty meters away from us, they both exited the vehicle, and I could clearly see they were armed with taser guns. "I am going to need your details Sir." The office tried again as we approached.

"Am I obliged to give you a name." I responded, answering with a question.

"No, you're not obliged." The officer replied with dismay in his voice. I grabbed my lad's arm and we just kept on walking. The two coppers looked at each other and one just shrugged his shoulders as we passed them. I kept looking back over my shoulder in case they got brave, but they just gave up and got back into their car. We headed one way, and they went the other way.

"That was good dad, I've never been stopped by them before." My lad said with a nervous smile on his face.

"Just remember son, if you haven't committed a crime then you have no business with them, you aren't obliged to give them any details and you have the right to remain silent, that means don't say a word, don't give a name because even that's illegal son." I replied.

"How can giving your name be illegal?" my son asked.

"Because the name you give them isn't yours, it's a legal name or a legal fiction name son. Me and your mom foolishly registered your birth because we thought we would be fined if we didn't. By registering your name that we lovingly chose for you we unwittingly created a fiction and gave ownership of you to the crown, but don't worry son, nobody owns you and nobody can take you away from me ever.

What they really on is the piece of paper they gave us called your birth certificate. We didn't know any of this at the time or we would have fought it mate. What they have done son is used your name to borrow millions of pounds from the bankers and they have pledged your future earnings as surety on the loan, but don't worry son, it's not just you, it's every man, woman and child they have enslaved with their scams. This is the fraud that me and thousands of other people are exposing mate. We are revealing their scams and standing up to their fake authority. We don't mean any harm to the policy enforcement officers, and if we must fight back then we usually just embarrass them, like I did with the sergeant earlier.

"But why do you call them policy enforcement officers instead of police?" The next question came. We still had about half a mile to walk so I took the opportunity to educate my lad.

"Because son, the government is a corporation, it's a business mate, it's not what we are led to believe it is. They keep passing or making up what they call laws but in fact they are just making up company policy. The police, who are a private company as well, then bully people into obeying these rules or polices. The people don't realize that they have the right to remove their consent to be governed and can say no to the nonsense rules of government.

Let's say that a politician or one of his mates has a company that produces steel. The politician makes up rules that only his steel, or steel from one of his mates can be sold in this country. Then he gets together with some other no-good politicians and makes it a law, then they get the police and other officials to go around and punish anyone who doesn't sell the politicians approved steel. This gives them the monopoly on the steel sales and nobody else gets a look in. Anybody who stands up to them is slated by the media, which of course is owned by their mates to." I took a few breaths, awaiting the next question, but it didn't come so I carried on talking.

"The policy enforcement officers can't force you to do anything that is against the law, so when they ask you for your name, which remember you don't own, then you are not obliged to give it to them if you haven't committed a crime. It's all a scam son, by their laws we are told we must send you for indoctrination in their public schools, where they fill your head full of nonsense for eleven or so years, so that you don't question them or stand up to them, but the tide is turning son.

We are starting to teach our children the truth. Anything you are forced to do against your will is null and void and fraud vitiates everything, which means when they trick you and you point it out to them, it should stop the validity of any claim they are making against you, so the fact that you haven't been told that it's illegal to use your legal name is fraud so that should be enough to put a stop to their nonsense, but they are all as corrupt as each other so if you ended up in court they would just make something up, just blatantly lie or change what you said by using legalese" I stopped talking for a second and awaited the next question.

"What's legalese?" came the next question, which was good as it meant he was listening.

"Legalese is a language used by lawyers and judge's son; it sounds exactly like the English language that we were taught, and speak every day, but they give different meanings to the words to trick you, for example, when a judge asks if you understand something, he is not saying do you comprehend what I am saying, he is asking if you stand under his authority. The correct response would be to say I don't stand under your authority, but I overstand you, meaning I comprehend what you are saying, and I know why you are saying it." I let out a sigh then continued. "It's all a con son, you got to court, expecting to get some sort of justice, but they just play a game with you, they trick you into being the name you don't own, then set up a trust in that name, they make themselves a beneficiary and you the trustee for the name you don't own, then make you pay for it. If that's not fraud then I don't know what is, sunshine." I answered as best as I could. I could already see the next question forming by the look on my lad's face.

"Why is it ok for them to do that dad?" he asked, looking puzzled.

"Well son, they are a law unto themselves. A long time ago a few men got together and decided, we need a few rules to keep things in order, and quite rightly so as you can't have people going around hurting innocent people, but what happened was a few, let's say well educated men, started giving themselves and their mates, imaginary powers and rights that we don't have, and if anybody questioned those powers then they got punished by the men with the fake powers. Basically, they would convince other people to hurt or kill the non-believers, so to prevent themselves from getting hurt the people went along with it, but soon, what started happening was the people with the imaginary powers started taking the piss. Instead of just punishing criminals, they realized by making lots of things illegal they could scam some money off people.

Now there is lawful and unlawful. Lawful means the act you are doing is ok to do and unlawful, means the act you are doing is not ok to do and these both fall under what is called common law, it's quite easy to remember common law son. Cause no harm, loss or injury, don't commit fraud and keep the peace. Basically, if there is no victim then there is no crime, but, and this is a big but, these men started making all sorts of stuff illegal so they could make money off it. If they wanted to son, they could make it illegal for me and you to walk down this road tonight, which is basically what they did with the covid curfews. They get the policy enforcement officers to force you to obey their rules and when you don't, they give them the power to issue fines, which is also unlawful because at one time only a judge could fine you in a court of law, and it had to be after a trial by jury, they changed the rules so anyone can bloody fine you now. They are even trying to stop your right to trial by jury now, which makes it even harder to get any justice in their unlawful courts." I was warming up now, with the alcohol and the exercise from walking. My lad was giving me a puzzled look, so I knew the next question was coming.

"Why did they come to Marks house tonight dad? I mean we were only having a good time; we didn't do anything wrong did we?" My lad asked with a worried tone to his voice.

"Don't worry son. Some nosey, good for nothing neighbor of Marks phoned the police because we had a party, they police thought they had a chance to make some money out of us and didn't expect to be confronted with people who overstand the rules. What we did tonight should be happening in every situation where the police get involved with innocent men and women. If you haven't requested their services, then have nothing to do with them. The copper who I choked out is just a man, he had no right whatsoever to try and hit me with that baton, he believes in his head he has power, and his mates and the people making up the rules believe he had the power to hit me for doing nothing wrong, but he was mistaken son. Don't be afraid to stand up to them, anybody who draws any weapon on you deserves a good beating and nobody can give you or anybody else the right to hurt another human being." I paused for a breath or two. We weren't far from home now so I slowed my pace down so we could talk more before we got back, and the computer took over my lad's mind again.

I didn't wait for a question this time, I just started talking. "The law, and government has been hijacked by criminal's son, and it's been that way for a long time. Fortunately, there are people fighting back, there is a very old document called the Magna Carta, that gives the people a way of taking back their power from these criminals. Its article sixty-one son and there are some men called barons, and these men enacted this article sixty-one, which is a security clause, on the twenty third of march, two thousand and one, this of course has been kept a secret by the government and the fake authorities because they would lose the imaginary control that they have and probably all end up jailed for treason. These good people are trying to fight back against the corporations." I paused for a breath or two.

"Why don't more people fight back?" my lad asked.

"Because they don't know that they can fight back, they don't even know that there's a problem. They truly believe whatever the news programs tell them and they trust the government, they will fight you for telling them anything different, most of them need to be governed son, most of them love giving seventy to eighty percent of their hard earned wages away every week and they don't even question it when another tax is introduced, and this is the other reason , they are living in fear of what this fictitious entity can do to them, all the people who work for government use fear to make you comply. They word their letters so people think that if they don't give in and obey the command or demand in the letter then they will be in even more trouble.

What people don't realize is that it is other men and women that are writing the letters. The government is just a word son, it's an idea, it can't write letters for itself, it requires men and women to bring it to life, so when they write a letter from a government entity or a corporation to your legal name, which if you remember I told you about earlier, then they require you to bring that legal name to life by responding. If all the men and women writing the letters realized what they were involved in, then I am sure most of them would be shocked.

The good news is the people are waking up and no longer living in fear. Even the ordinary people who watch the news and normally just keep paying and slaving away every week are starting to wake up, they are starting to see it's a scam. The government creates a problem that doesn't exist, then bombards the people with it, next they get the people to react in fear to the problem and demand that something be done, then they sell you the solution if you will just give them more money or allow them to make up some more rules. It's a scam son, a massive scam. Every copper I deal with, who walks away empty handed because they haven't tricked me into doing business, makes it easier for you and your generation to say no too, and even easier for your kids if you choose to make me a grandad.

Every time one of us goes to court and stands over and not under the judge's fake authority, then it makes it better for everyone else. Every time we remove our consent from their bullshit, we win a little battle. Every time we deny them life for the legal fiction, we beat them. Their days are numbered son. I am going to teach you as much as I can but there is still a mountain, I have got to learn myself, but a golden rule is that you have to lose the fear. That is their favorite weapon. They convince you that you will be in more trouble if you don't play along, if you don't answer for the dead entity they created, if you don't give life to the fiction then you will be punished even more, well fuck them son, we are not fictions, we are living men and women, we are the highest authority over ourselves whilst we are in this realm. Lose the fear of what another man can do to you, and you are nearly there so if you lose the fear of what a fictional entity can do to you then you have won. There are people sitting in jail for spreading the truth and its wrong son." I sighed loudly as I stopped talking.

"Will we win dad?" my lad asked.

"We are on the side of good son, so we have already won. It's just a formality now mate. The last few pieces of the puzzle are coming together. The cowards are going into hiding. They think their friends and their secret societies with people in high places can keep them safe, but the knowledge is spreading so fast that there is nothing they can do. The men and women want proof of the imaginary authority that these parasites claim to have, but there is no authority to prove son, just other people's belief or fear. They can have you thrown in jail but if the man doing the jailing realizes he is being screwed over by them to, he will eventually lose the fear and say "No." If the copper realizes he is tricking people into doing business he may say "No." If the soldier realizes he is being used to steal a country's wealth and he is not freeing, but helping to oppress the people on foreign shores, then he may say "No." there is nothing to fear son." I replied as I pulled my lad in close and hugged him, ruffling his hair for good measure.

We rounded the corner of the alley way that leads onto our road, and we walked the last fifty meters to our house in silence. There was no longer any need to check over my shoulder as we walked up the short path to the house as a sense of peace was descending on everyone. The information that was up until a few days ago only known by a few was now becoming common knowledge. People like my lad who could upload information to the web then disappear just as quick were filling the social media sites with the truth faster than the government could make up knew lies.

Average people were talking about the fraud that is being committed by the councils and the courts, even the police were starting to question what they were involved in. I smiled as I thought about the significance of the last week, and especially Saturday's rally and the arrests of the policy enforcement officers.

The key turned easily in the lock and the door swung inwards and the smell of home filled my nostrils. My lad disappeared upstairs as fast as he could, no doubt some imaginary battle needed winning. I pushed the front door shut and threw the bolt over then headed for the kitchen. I poured a larger than usual glass of whiskey, the slumped heavily, into the settee to enjoy my nightcap. No doubt there would be some sort of backlash from the parasites, but you must expect that when you're fighting evil.

11

"If you want a picture of the future, imagine a boot stamping on a human face forever."
George Orwell 1984

The day started like most of my Sundays, with a bacon sandwich and a cup of coffee. It is my intention to do as little as possible today, after the busy day I had yesterday, and as I have enough food and drink in the house, I can spend the day in the sanctuary that is my garden. The weather is being kind for September and although there are a few clouds in the sky they all seem natural and not the man-made chemical clouds that the airplanes spray. My lad is busy on his computer and to my surprise he is not on games for a change, but he is watching videos on common law and dealing with the bullshit.

My lad shouted from the bathroom window for me to come up stairs and watch something. I heaved myself out of the swinging garden chair, headed inside through the back door, i climbed the stairs and headed along the landing to my lad's room. "Dad have a look at this, it's from a rally yesterday." he said excitedly.

"Let's have a look then mate." I said as I leant down towards the computer screen.

"Look at the police, they are getting handcuffed by the people." He was laughing as he spoke.

"Its good son, the people are starting to stand up for themselves, and by the look of it nobody was harmed." I replied, then immediately spotted the familiar cap and coat that I was wearing as on the screen, I pulled a copper to the ground but luckily the cap had done its job, and my face was covered by the peak.

"Look Dad there's a news report about it." My lad gushed enthusiastically.

"Turn the sound up mate." I said, eager to hear the lies that the reporter would come up with.

"And in Bringham today, we have our reporter, Martin Coles, Martin what's going on down there?" The announcer said as he handed over to the reporter.

"Well John, I am in the main square in Bringham, at an organized rally protesting against the government and the police's handling of the vaccine passport requirements. The speakers are giving talks, claiming the government is unlawful and they are basing this on very old laws and something to do with the Magna Carta, which we have quickly checked out with our legal experts, and they assure us this is just another conspiracy theory."

The reporter played his part brilliantly and lied through his teeth. The announcer asked another prescript question. "And what have the police done to break up this unlawful gathering and to stop these lies being spread Martin?"

I was glued to the screen, "How were they going to get out of this then?" I thought to myself. The camera quickly cut to some footage that must have been filmed in the winter. The people getting arrested in the footage were wearing woolly hats and warm coats, and there was even water from rain on the ground. The crafty bastards were showing footage of a different rally.

The reporter started talking but off camera. "The police did an excellent job of breaking up the crowd and several arrests were made. The main speakers and several protestors were arrested and will be charged with public order offences." The camera cut back to the reporter now standing in the dry, empty square, and the bullshit was complete. The news clip ended there.

My son attached the real footage of the day's events to the fake footage and reposted it, then immediately deleted the account he had created. Hopefully enough people would see the two bits of footage and realize the truth. Within ten minutes there were over a thousand likes on the video and the number was climbing by the second. I watched my lad do a mix of the footage from Australia and the footage from the rally yesterday. He posted it in the comments from the last video, being careful to cover his tracks. The comments said it all really. There was nobody who trusted the mainstream media and no support for the government or the police. I ruffled my lad's hair as I walked out of the bedroom then headed for the garden for a couple of hours rest before I paid a visit to church tonight.

I sat back in the garden chair and opened my book to the marked page and started reading. This was my escape from reality for an hour or two. At some point I must have stopped reading and nodded off. The warm sunny afternoon with clear skies had been replaced with a chemtrail sky. The long streaks of filth had done their job and spread out across the whole sky, creating a hazy blanket. This was all part of the climate change agenda that the government has been creating for several years now. It's just something else that they have created, and of course if we give them enough money and we are willing to lose a load of freedom then they can save us from the problem they are creating. Same old, same old. They create the problem, get a reaction from the public, then offer a solution for a cost, and that's how it works every time. Hopefully the people are waking up enough not to fall for it but unfortunately there are some people who believe what the mainstream media and the papers tell them.

My lad popped his head around the back corner of the shed and announced he had two hundred thousand likes, and thirty thousand comments on the video he had posted. I smiled as he excitedly told me about some of the stuff he had found, and I promised to take a look later but for now it was time to get ready for tonight.

The shower water did its job and woke me up. Feeling refreshed, I dried myself, put on some fresh clothes and said "Bye."

To my lad before heading downstairs to put my boots on. I opened the front door and stepped out onto the short blue brick path, taking several deep breaths of the cool evening air as I shut the door behind me.

As I rounded the corner into the street where the church is, I was greeted by a police car and three policy enforcement officers. This was not unusual now as it was easier to make money out of people with unlawful curfew fines and vaccine status checks, than it was catching criminals.

I knew they would stop me, and although it would have been easier to turn around and go to the church another way it would have meant they had won, so I carried on in their direction. I walked at a steady pace towards them and took several deep breaths as I got closer. I was walking in the road to the side of them as they occupied the pavement. The old lady they were harassing was putting the green vaccine pass back into her purse as she started to walk away. They had failed to scare her or make any money so no doubt I would be their next victim.

"Excuse me sir." The nearest copper said as I was nearly level with him.

"Not tonight thank you." I replied as I walked past. He darted past me and blocked my way, closely followed by his two mates.

"When a police officer talks to you, you should stop and do as your told sir." He started with his nonsense.

"Number one sunshine, I am not a sir, and number two, I have no business with you or the corporation you work for, now unless you suspect me of committing a crime, I suggest you move out of my way." I replied firmly.

"When a police officer order's you to stop, you must stop." He tried again.

"Did you just order me to do something constable? Orders are chargeable. Now if you want me to stop and converse with you, I will charge you the sum of twenty thousand pounds. I will give you a moment to retract your order." I replied again.

"But." He stammered.

"There are no buts, constable. If you order a pizza or a new coat, you pay for your order, otherwise you are in dishonor or a debtor constable, now you are ordering me to stop and converse with you, if so, I will require twenty thousand pounds from you if I carry out that order." I replied, staring straight into his eyes. He glanced around at his two colleagues who just shrugged their shoulders as their mate dug himself a deeper hole.

"Can I just get your name mate?" He tried again.

"Name; I don't use names constable, am I obliged to give you a name?" I responded, playing with him now.

"When I ask you for your details, you have to give them to me." He lied nervously.

"Think back to your training constable, remember the case law, Rice verses Conolly, ring any bells?" I quoted case law that he would have been taught at copper school.

"I, erm, you're not obliged to give a name, and I'm not ordering anything." He stammered.

I smiled and said "Good, for a moment there I thought you wanted to give me money and you were encouraging me to commit crown copyright theft by using a legal name constable. Now unless you have any objections, I will go about my evening, unhindered by you" He immediately moved aside and I walked off smiling, thinking "That's another little victory."

As I walked through the doors of the small spiritualist church, the familiar old building smell filled my nose. Eric, the elderly gent on the door greeted me with a smile and a nod as he handed me a hymn book. I headed for my usual seat, and I was soon joined by Mark and his wife. There was no need for secret messages or passing bits of paper back and forth as we just didn't care, the information was online now, and as fast as the authorities took it down someone reposted it.

"Good night last night Dan?" Mark said with a wink.

"Very good mate, we got stopped on the way back, but we soon fobbed them off." I replied.

"What do you think of David?" Mark asked.

"Seems legit enough Mark, how do you know him?" I responded.

"He works with the missus. He was telling the whole office about the Magna Carta, and the wife thought we would like to meet him." Mark said quietly as the church was starting to fill up.

"And what about the other events of the evening?" I said, referring to the visit by the policy enforcement officers.

“Well, there will be a fine in the post addressed to THE LEGAL OCCUPIER, and of course that’s not me, so I will just return it to sender or put it in the bin. There’s no point giving any life to a letter addressed to a fictional character. Well, I’m pretty sure a copper can’t fine you and there are no courts of law in this country anymore, just administrative courts and I haven’t been in front of any jury.” Mark replied almost laughing.

“Are you still ok for tomorrow night?” I asked, remembering the tickets that David had given us the night before.

“Yes kidda, I just hope it’s not just the usual hand-picked audience asking pre-scripted questions.” Mark replied.

“Well even if it is we may get to ask at least one awkward question.” I shrugged as I answered.

The Sunday service began with a couple of songs from the hymn book, which certainly raised a smile or two, as I mentioned before these were not religious hymns but popular songs. The lady speaker fumbled with the cd player between tracks making another smile creep across my face. With the lord's prayer recited whilst standing up and a loud "Amen" at the end, the service was ready to start.

Sally, the lovely lady speaker was scanning the room and eventually settled her gaze on a young lady at the front of the room. The young lady sat mesmerized as the medium gave her evidence, and by the sound of it she was spot on. The young lady wiped away tears between giving answers confirming what the medium was getting through was correct. As the medium bought the message to a close the young lady thanked her, and a smile returned to her face.

Sally scanned the room again, and to my surprise her eyes fell on me. "The man there in the green coat. Can you take a man in spirit, and I want to say grandad?" she asked, barely giving me time to answer with a nod. “This gentleman is proudly showing me his medals, so he must have fought in the war. He says you are fighting a battle of your own at the moment. He says don’t worry you are not alone, and every battle is a little victory, he says you will win if you stay on the side of good. He is showing me a crowd of people and a stage. He is repeating the word truth, he is saying speak the truth, and he is showing me a victory parade. Take his love and the message, God bless.” And with that she moved on to the next soul who needed to hear something that night.

I sat smiling, and I got a little thumbs up from Mark, sitting next to me as this seemed to confirm the message I’d had earlier in the week. Sally gave several more messages then brought the service to a close. We sang another popular song and recited the closing prayer.

The ladies of the church busied themselves in the little kitchen at the rear of the building, quickly producing about forty cups of tea. Me and mark stood chatting about the message and getting a few ideas together for tomorrow's meeting with the parasites. After finishing our cups of tea and munching on a couple of biscuits we returned our cups to the tea trolly, said good night to Eric the elderly doorman and stepped out into the now chilly evening air.

A quick glance down the road revealed the same policy enforcement officers from earlier, harassing a few of the people who had left before us. They were probably checking the vaccine status or carbon scores of their victims. New company policy as of yesterday was that your booster shots had to be up to date and clearly marked on your vaccine passport if you wanted to go about your life without harassment. This is adding more urgency to our truth speaking mission.

Mark saw me shaking my head at the nonsense going on and said "Come on, I'll give you a lift. It'll save you getting into any bother."

“Fair play mate.” I responded as me, Mark and his wife headed for the car. Once inside we put our seat belts on, and Mark started the engine. I sat behind Marks wife who had moved the passenger seat forward to give me as much room as possible. If we had to get out it would mean the coppers would need to split up to deal with both of us on opposite sides of the car.

We had no choice but to head in their direction, but hopefully they would have scammed enough money off the people on foot and would leave us alone. As we got to within about forty meters of them, one of them broke away from the others and stepped into the road and raised his arm, gesturing for Mark to stop the car. Mark obeyed the command, at the same time as pressing the central locking button, securing all the doors on the car. Mark brought the car to a stop about five meters away from the copper, meaning the officer had to come to us. Mark rolled the window down one inch, just enough to hear and be heard, but a small enough gap to prevent car keys being grabbed by these criminals.

"Good evening, Sir." He started with his nonsense. "We are checking the vaccine status and carbon output of people who are in the area tonight, to make sure nobody is breaking the new laws regarding unvaccinated movement after seven pm."

Mark glanced around at me and smiled, he turned straight back to the copper and said without hesitation, "What the fuck are you talking about, Laws, there are no laws regarding this nonsense constable. You are acting as a police constable this evening, aren't you? Or are you acting as a company policy enforcement officer?" The copper didn't quite know what to say.

"I, erm, well" was all he could get out of his mouth before mark told him some truth's.

"This nonsense that they have you forcing onto us is not law constable, it's just some rules for their own little game that they are playing out. They are playing the vaccine game at the moment with a little bit of climate change thrown in. Next week they will start a war with someone. I bet you won't be out arresting soldiers for being out unvaccinated after seven o'clock, shooting innocent men and women in other countries. How about if they decide that the unvaccinated aren't allowed to buy food next week because they made a new rule for their game, will you stop people eating constable or do you have a little bit of common sense? Can you not see what they have you doing constable? You are stealing money for a corporation, so its profits are up, and the shareholders are getting paid. Where is your duty inspector tonight? Let's have him out here right now constable. In fact, I might arrest you myself for forcing statutes onto nonconsenting men and women. I'm pretty sure what you are doing is piracy, or even better you can all arrest each other for manipulation, deceit, fraud, kidnap, assault and downright dishonesty. Now I am leaving." And with that Mark put the window back up and pulled off. The copper just stood there open mouthed as we drove off.

"You forgot harassment." I said jokingly.

Mark slammed the breaks on, opened the window thrust his head out the best he could and shouted, "I forgot to add harassment."

I was crying with laughter in the back of the car. I was sorry that the journey was only about another fifty meters as Mark had rounded the corner into my road.

We pulled up outside my house and I said, "Good night, love you both, thank you." Through tears of laughter. "See you tomorrow kidda." Came Marks reply.

12

"Civil disobedience is not our problem. Our problem is civil obedience. Our problem is that people all over the world have obeyed the dictates of leaders. Millions have been killed because of this obedience. Our problem is that people are obedient all over the world in the face of poverty, starvation, stupidity, war and cruelty. Our problem is that people are obediently filling our jails full of petty thieves while the grand thieves are running our country. That's our problem."
Howard Zinn

The day passed slowly at work; I couldn't concentrate as I was going through the questions in my head for tonight's little meeting with the politicians. I got home for about four thirty, showered and ate tea with my lad. Mark will be picking me up at six pm for the short journey into town. In the meantime, I was pacing the floor, the adrenaline tightening my stomach. I felt like I was preparing for a physical fight, but hopefully there wouldn't be any violence tonight.

At five fifty-five I slipped my jacket on, checking my pockets to make sure I had no government id on me, no driver's license, no bank cards and definitely no mobile phone. I secured my keys into the zip up pocket on my coat, shouted "Bye." To my lad and stepped outside into the cool evening air. The sun was giving off the last of its heat for the day and there was a tinge of red in the sky.

Marks car came into view around the slight curve in the road to the right of me. I moved forward, stepped off the curb and pulled the handle on the passenger side of the now stationary car.

“Alright kidda.” Came the familiar greeting from Mark.

“How’s it going?” I responded as I ducked my head and got into the passenger seat. I fumbled with the seat belt that had somehow got stuck behind the seat but eventually I won, and the belt clicked into place.

“How are you doing? Are you ready for this?” Mark asked as we pulled off.

“I’m as ready as I’ll ever be. how about you?” I replied.

“I’m good mate, and I have been looking forward to this all day. It’s a live broadcast but there’s a five second delay in case they want to cut anything. I’m hoping if we are clever enough that we can get at least a bit of information out there.” Mark replied, watching the road as he spoke.

"We will be fine mate, and if they do cut us off at least we will have tried." I reassured Mark.

We pulled onto the large car park at the top of the town, Mark pulled the car into a parking bay, and I got out to look for the ticket machine. I returned two minutes and nearly £5 lighter as I had allowed four hours for our evening out. I voiced my dismay at the parking charge, but Mark just laughed. "Never mind that mate, we have bigger fish to fry."

We headed out of the car park and into the pedestrianized part of the town where the only shops still open were the takeaways, the smell of the various foods combining to make a pungent aroma. This would lure the hardcore drinkers at closing time from the few pubs that were scattered about the town.

We headed down a small passageway and passed the bus terminal, each bus arriving or departing with only a handful of people on board. We rounded the corner of the road that the town hall was located on, and we were greeted with a host of outside broadcast vans, not just the local stations but a couple of national ones too. The politicians think they are putting on a show tonight, but we had a show of our own planned.

We joined the que at the public entrance of the large stone building, which is carved with symbols and coats of arms, commemorative foundation stones ran along the front of the hall. I read a couple whilst we were queuing. THIS STONE WAS LAID BY THE RIGHT HONOURABLE MEMBER OF PARLIAMENT SIR CYRIL EDWARDS IN 1844. The next stone was laid by THE GOOD LADY MAYORESS MRS H. JENKINS and so on and so forth. I wondered if Sir Cyril Edwards was really honorable or if he was as corrupt as the shower of shit we have now.

Soon it was our turn at the front of the que, Mark handed the two printed conformation emails to the doorman, who scanned the bar codes. He patted us down to check for weapons and we had to walk through a metal detector at the entrance. Despite having to go through twice as my keys, and belt buckle set it off, we passed the security checks unhindered. As we entered the foyer, which was adorned with paintings of the many mayors and mayoresses that had graced the building in years gone by, I caught a glimpse of a few familiar faces. "Maybe we have some back up mate." I said to Mark as I nodded in the direction of a couple we knew well. Mark just smiled in response.

We were ushered through a large double wooden door and into the main assembly hall, this too was very ornate, with a huge chandelier hanging from the beautifully painted ceiling, and various plaques and rolls of honor hanging on the walls. The usual capacity of this place is around three hundred people, but that had been greatly reduced judging by the spaces between each seat. It looked like they were putting on a show for the covidiots, who would undoubtedly turn up with masks, gloves and bubble wrap suits.

The seats weren't numbered or predesignated, so we just settled for a couple of seats about midway along the hall and slightly to the right of center. We both made a mental note of where the fire exits were in case it went tits up tonight and we had to leave in a hurry.

I removed my coat before I sat down and hung it on the back of the chair. I reached down and picked up the complimentary bottle of water and program that was on the floor beneath my seat. The program gave a brief introduction of the people speaking and answering questions tonight.

I glanced around at all the camera and sound people, busying themselves with last-minute checks and testing light levels. A look at the large clock on the wall above the stage area revealed we only had half an hour until the show started. I looked over at Mark who was reading his free program, he pointed at a name on the thin glossy piece of paper. Amongst the legal fiction names of the politicians and other guests, there was a single word. I leaned in closer and read the name that Mark was pointing to, it just read Sarah. I smiled to myself, if this was Sarah from the rally on Saturday then the politicians would be in for a shock. I leaned back in my chair and started to silently go through the questions and responses I might need shortly.

Fifteen minutes to go and one of the parasites entered the stage and took their seat. The place was as full as it was going to get tonight, and the large wooden entrance doors were pulled too. More people came onto the stage guided by members of the production crew and took the seats they were directed to. Make-up people did the finishing touches on the guests' faces and their chairs were raised or lowered to give them all the appearance of the same physical presents. A sound engineer adjusted the microphone on the necktie of the politician on the right. Water was poured into the glasses that sat on the low table in the middle of the group. Finally, a member of the crew addressed us in the audience.

"Ladies and gents, we will be going live in five minutes. Can I just ask you all to remain silent whilst we do the introductions, then when we ask for questions, please raise your hand and wait for the presenter to come to you. Please wait for the sound engineer to put the large boom microphone over your head so we can all hear you and please state which guest you are directing your question to. Just a reminder, please check your mobile phones are switched completely off as they will interfere with our broadcast and of course please don't use foul or derogatory language" The crew member paused for breath.

"Two minutes;" another technician shouted over the top of him.

"Please refrain from heckling or shouting over the top of each other and again remember to wait for the microphone or we will only partly hear your questions." He continued.

"One minute;" the technician shouted. "Right, silence please, thirty seconds;" he shouted as he exited the stage.

I watched as a member of the crew counted down from five silently with his fingers so the presenter could see. Five, four, three, two, one and two thumbs up signaled that we were on the air.

"Good evening, ladies and gentlemen, I'm Richard Jones, and this is Talk Time, coming live from Walson town hall, and our guests tonight are the right honorable Edward Higgins MP and health secretary for the conservative party."

The presenter motioned in the direction of the grey-haired, red-faced man to his left, who nodded in the general direction of the audience as a polite round of applause was given.

"And to my right we have Mrs. Mary Fellows, local labor MP and shadow health secretary." The presenter moved his hand slightly to the right in the direction of the rather stern looking woman wearing a business suit, she in turn nodded towards us in the audience, and again a polite round of applause was given. The presenter continued, "Also joining us is Simon Williams, a local business owner, Sarah, a representative of the truth movement, and finally, Chief super intendant Rodger Jacobs from west Mainland police." The presenter gestured to each person in turn as he spoke. Another short and respectful round of applause was given by the audience.

"In light of recent events with vaccine passports, lock downs, carbon output checks and all manner restrictions of being placed on certain members of the public, we will be asking our MP's and other guests questions about these policies. Edward Higgins, can I start with you?" the politician just nodded slightly as a response." Can you justify the restrictions placed on unvaccinated people in entertainment venues, workplaces and even supermarkets?" The host started the ball rolling.

"Yes, I think we can justify the restrictions. If your unvaccinated you pose a risk to the vaccinated people who have done their bit to stop the spread of the virus. Why should you be going about spreading the virus potentially infecting people." The politician gave his pre scripted answer.

"Hang on Mr. Higgins, but the vaccine doesn't stop you contracting the virus, it supposedly just lessons the effects of the illness, so how do the unvaccinated pose a risk to the vaccinated?" the host fired back at the politician.

"We have done research to prove the unvaccinated pose a risk and scientists say," he was cut short by the host again.

"Scientists that you fund agree with you, but its independent scientists that have reported that the vaccine doesn't stop you getting the virus and doesn't stop you transmitting the virus, so what difference does it make if an unvaccinated man goes for a drink with a vaccinated man when the outcome could be the same?" the host said firmly.

"The government has the right to impose restrictions as it sees fit, and we will enforce these restrictions using every power that we have" The politician replied defensively.

"This doesn't justify the removal of people's rights to go about their lives without hinderance every five minutes from the police, and it certainly doesn't justify the fines that the police are giving out." The host stepped in again.

"When we were voted into power, we took over the right to make these decisions. Our powers can be extended during times of national emergency" the politician replied weakly.

I took the opportunity to raise my hand. I must have caught the attention of the host as he came straight to me. "let's hear from the audience. The man there in the blue top." He said referring to me.

"Mr. Higgins, in the last two comments you made, you used the word POWER three times. I think this is misleading as when the people who are foolish enough to vote and consent to being governed, vote, then they are voting you into service, not power, you are a public servant and you and your colleagues are here to serve us not to dictate what we can and can't do. Now the power that you think you have requires the consent of the governed, so if a man or woman says no to one of your nonsense rules then there is nothing you can do." I finished speaking and a small round of applause came from the rest of the audience.

"That's nonsense, we erm, we have the power to make laws that protect people and," he stammered but I cut him off.

"There's that word power again Mr. Higgins, you have no power over any living man or woman. You may believe you do, and it's obvious that you all act like you do but in reality, it's the people who have the ultimate power. We are your employers; we employ you and your colleagues to run things. If any of us in this room did our jobs as badly or as incompetently as you lot have over the past sixty or seventy years, then we would be sacked. You create the problems of this world with your under handed dealings and your secretive little scams, then make out that you're saving us from some problem that you created. Answer me this Mr. Higgins, if these restrictions are to protect us all, why were you out partying with other politicians during the height of this nonsense?" I replied, staring him straight in the eye.

"We have already started an investigation into the parties, and it seems we may have made mistakes. But we are working on fixing the problem." He answered weakly.

"You are investigating yourselves Mr. Higgins, and no doubt you will all get a little £50 fine and brush it all under the carpet.

We were all locked down, vaccinated and unvaccinated people, locked in their houses and told we would kill our granny if we went to visit her, but you lot were out partying." The host fired into the politician.

"We will pay the fines and we have already apologized. We were just blowing off steam." His response angered the audience and several loud shouts echoed through the room.

"Mr. Higgins, you are missing the point. What did you know that you weren't telling the public? If you and your friends felt safe enough to have a party where there was dancing, hugging and drinking going on, then why were we still forbid by law to leave our houses?" the host added.

"We are looking into it at the moment and if any laws were broken then we will be more than willing to pay the fines." He added weakly.

"Mrs. Fellows were you at the party back in May?" the host directed his question towards the other politician.

"No, I was not, but I'm sure as Mr. Higgins has already stated. If the rules were broken, then they will pay the fines." She responded thinking paying a fine justified the politicians' actions.

"Mrs. Fellows you weren't at the party in May, but you were caught visiting your friends two hundred miles away from your home across the border in Wales;" the host caught her in his little trap.

"I have already been through this with the party chairman, and my friend had been recently widowed and needed support. I acted as any good friend would and went to console her." Came the lame response.

Several hands shot up in the air, and the host gestured towards a young lady near the back of the room. "The young lady with the white shirt."

"Mrs. Fellows my mother lay dying of cancer in a hospital on her own. Without any of her loved ones around her. Despite me proving I didn't have the virus and pleading with the nurses to be allowed to see her, I was told to go home, and the hospital would notify me when she had passed. Now you sit there and basically dismiss your actions as those of a concerned friend. Your friend's husband passed away twelve months before any of this started. We can read Mrs. Fellows, your little secret has been all over social media today, your injunction against the newspapers worked but your attempts at secrecy failed regarding the internet." The lady had her say, just about holding back the tears.

The host saved the politician from any more embarrassment by moving on. "Can we come to Mr. Simon Williams. Mr. Williams can you give us an idea of how the lock downs have affected you, and have you started to recover financially from these new laws?"

"Well Richard I own a small family business, making and selling glassware, we employ eighteen people locally and use the services of several local businesses. These laws have been devastating for us and our employees. Far from protecting anybody the new restrictions are crippling us. I am now required to demand my staff get an experimental injection if they want to earn a living. These men and women are highly skilled and hard to come by. The decision by half my team to say no to being Guiney pigs for this is affecting us all financially and emotionally. We all work together as a team, but these laws have driven a wedge between people who have worked together for, in some cases, twenty-five years. I have had to tell some of my staff to stay at home at the moment, and because they are being classed as making themselves unemployable, they are getting no financial help from the government, and coupled with the new climate carbon emissions bill, things are getting harder" Simon's sorrow showed in his voice.

"Let's go to the audience" Richard the presenter scanned the audience for raised hands and pointed straight at Mark next to me. "The Gentleman with the brown jacket." Mark waited for the sound man to put the microphone above him.

"Can I ask to see the vaccine passports of the politicians please? As it's now a law then I'm sure you won't mind" Mark gestured with his hand towards the stage.

"Yes, I agree" The host said as he turned towards the guests. "It's now required by your laws so let's see those little cards" The two politicians glanced at each other.

"My vaccine status is between me and my doctor, its private and I am not willing to share that sort of medical information here tonight" Mr. Higgins pipped up straight away.

"Mr. Higgins, you have made a supposed law that states we the people must provide vaccine status cards as of next week to gain entry to shops, entertainment venues and in some cases as Simon just said, employment, so your vaccine status is not between you and your doctor, it's now required by your own laws that you show us." Mark fired into the politician.

"I, erm due to security reasons I am allowed to keep that information private as a matter of secrecy." The politician squirmed at his own words.

The host had a look of amazement on his face and the audience muttered loudly. "Mrs. Fellows do you have your vaccine card with you. Can you prove you've had the vaccine that is slowly becoming necessary just to live?" the presenter asked.

"I am not willing to discuss my medical information in front of millions of people on television." She replied arrogantly.

"Sarah, can we come to you please?" the host gestured to the young lady sitting facing the politicians. "Firstly, can I ask why you don't use a sir name?"

"I am commonly called Sarah, I have a family name which is private, Richard. It is the use of these crown corporation owned, legal fiction names that is helping to enslave all of you. None of you own the names you are using to do business, and therefore you are committing theft by using them. It would take the whole show for me to explain this, so I suggest the people watching do some research." Sarah replied but was cut short by the politician.

"Excuse me young lady," But that was as far as he got.

"Don't young lady me and don't you dare interrupt me when I am talking. I pay your wages Mr. Higgins." She stopped the politician in his tracks. "I am at the forefront of the battle for the truth. Me and thousands of men and women have had enough of the lies, deceit and treachery of the people we pay to serve us. The fake laws that you are making up to trick people into giving you money are unlawful. Your use of deceit, force, coercion and in some cases violence are unconstitutional. All your nonsense requires the consent of the people. You seem to have forgotten this and the people have forgotten this too. I am here to remind everyone that we have ancient laws that protect us from what is going on at the moment, laws based on our customs and traditions. Our political system has been hijacked by criminals. This isn't just about a vaccine or a virus. It's not about emissions and carbon. It's about the systematic removal of our rights and the erosion of truth. You two have no power over anybody." Sarah pointed at the two open-mouthed politicians. "And you Chief inspector have no right whatsoever to order the people under your command to force anything onto anyone." Sarah stopped talking and leaned back in her chair.

The host gestured towards the female politician who seemed a little shocked at Sarah's bluntness." Would you like to comment on that Mrs. Fellows?"

"Utter nonsense. The laws we are enacting are for the benefit of everyone, they are not for making money. We don't need the people's permission to do the things that we as your elected representatives see fit. It's people like you that spout nonsense that hinders us in creating our vision. You mentioned a constitution, we are not American Sarah, we don't have a constitution." The politician snapped back.

"We have the Magna carta of 1215, Mrs. Fellows. I'm sure the corporation you work for would be happy if it didn't exist. We also have the bill of rights of 1689. The true laws of this land are the common laws, and we only break those when we harm others, damage their property, steal what is not ours or commit fraud in our business dealings. Statutes, acts, mandates and bills are drawn up and passed by parliament as legislation. Legislation has power over us only if we consent to it. The rules and regulations defined by your statutes are said in law dictionaries to acquire the force of law only when we give our consent. The fact that we are all sovereign means we can withhold or withdraw our consent and that should be the end of the matter. The state knows this to be true, but it would prefer it if it was kept secret.

We are all born sovereign Mrs. fellows and to be sovereign is to have absolute authority over ourselves. The state tries to dismiss the Magna Carta, it makes us look the other way, it tries to convince us that the power of the document is gone. The truth is that the law of the land is older than parliament. The Magna Carta reaffirms the ancient common laws and was sealed before your parliament even existed Mrs. Fellows. It is beyond your remit, the unwritten constitution that Magna Carta speaks of, is out of your parliament's reach. Parliament, the government and the state are creations of human beings and therefore are subordinate and beneath us, it should serve us not rule us." Sarah finished talking and reached forward for the glass of water in front of her.

There was no reply from the open-mouthed politicians. The audience kept a respectful silence as they were enjoying the slow but sure destruction of the politician's imaginary power. The host stepped in before they dug themselves a deeper hole. "Can I ask what you have done for your constituents during the height of this Mrs. Fellows."

"I personally attended a vaccine center and helped out." Mrs. Fellows started to speak. I raised my hand and caught the hosts' attention.

"The gentleman there," Richard pointed straight at me.

"Mrs. Fellow you attended a vaccine center for a photo opportunity at the height of the pandemic. Me and the rest of the population were told to stay in the house because of fears we would kill everyone. We were told by the chief medical adviser to the government that anybody who isn't a critical worker must not leave the house, but you took yourself and a photographer into a vaccine center. Putting yourself, your family and the photographer at risk. You then posted the evidence on social media, so my question is this. Was this essential work?"

"As a politician we have to be seen taking to the front line when there is a crisis, and I thought doing my bit and helping out was the right thing to do." she answered weakly.

"That's fair enough, I admire your dedication but why did you need to take a photographer with you?" I asked, suppressing a smile.

"I wanted the public to see that I was making an effort." She replied but with no real conviction.

"I thought you would be safer in your house; I mean you awarded yourselves ten thousand pounds each to set up an office at home when this nonsense started. Do you think ten thousand pounds is a little excessive for a laptop and a chair?" I got a glare from the politician and a cheer from the audience.

Richard the presenter saved her from any more embarrassment by moving on. “In light of the recent energy crisis, can I ask you Mr. Higgins what your party is doing to ensure prices don’t rise again with winter only around the corner?”

“We have met several times with the energy providers and unfortunately if prices need to be raised then that is what will happen. The energy providers cannot lose money, so they have to increase prices based on global fluctuations in the market.” The politician parroted the usual nonsense.

“Mr. Higgins, the energy providers as you call them provide absolutely nothing except a bill for something that should belong to all of us. They are energy brokers not providers and the fact that they have trebled their profits for doing nothing is an example of the greed of a few people amongst us. There were people choosing whether to feed themselves or keep warm last winter.

This of course does not affect you due to the amount of money you choose to pay yourselves. I doubt that you went hungry or cold last winter." Sarah held the politicians gaze as she spoke.

"The government provided help for every household in the form of grants. There was money from the government to help with the cost-of-living crisis." The politician replied weakly.

"The cost-of-living crisis as you put it was engineered by you and your colleagues Mr. Higgins. The gas, water and electricity bills could have been discharged with the correct paperwork, you know this, your colleagues know this, and the energy brokers know this, and you all fear the day we all realise what you are up to." Sarah had the politician fixed in her sights.

"I'm not sure what you mean young lady?" the politician looked worried as he spoke.

"You know exactly what discharging the debt is Mr. Higgins and it has been conveniently hidden from us. For the benefit of the audience, I will explain. Some of you will remember the old bills we used to get, the top part was the bill or liability and the bottom third that looked like a cheque was the remedy. If you ever bothered to read it, it had the words, BANK GIRO CREDIT printed on it. They were crediting you something. If the bill was for £250 then the amount on the cheque at the bottom was £250. By filling out the cheque correctly and posting it back to them the debt would be discharged. you cannot take the cheque to the bank and cash it, but you can discharge the bill or debt with it. We in our ignorance took it to the post office and handed over our hard-earned money because we thought we were liable for the debt but in fact as I am sure the politicians, bankers and energy brokers know, there is nothing to pay the debt with. Our money is debt, it is an IOU, just a promise to pay and you cannot pay a debt with a debt. By paying theses bills with cash, you are compounding the debt and adding to the imaginary national debt, by discharging the debt you would be doing everyone a favour.” Sarah paused for a sip of water.

“Utter nonsense young lady. Money is not debt. You pay your debts with money, or you face the consequences.” The politician barked back.

“Mr. Higgins the pieces of plastic money in our pockets are worthless promissory notes, they are IOU’s. There is no gold or silver backing these pieces of plastic up.” Sarah pulled a £10 note from her trouser pocket and held it in the air.

“The only thing giving this any value is our belief in its value. The only thing this is backed up by is our labour. We create the energy that gives this value. We are the creditors Mr. Higgins, we the people create all of this and you and people like you take it from us.” Sarah was now baiting the MP, leading him into her next trap.

“Young lady, you are mistaken. The banks create the money and lend it out to people in the form of loans and mortgages." The politician glared at Sarah as he spoke.

"It is you that is mistaken Mr. Higgins. We are the creditors. The money is created when we sign the mortgage or loan agreement. The agreements are promissory notes. By signing the agreement, we promise to pay the bearer the sum of x number of pounds with interest and of course the only way we can do that is by working ourselves to death to pay back something that we created out of thin air." Sarah waited for the politician to reply but the host stepped in and changed the subject.

"Let's come to chief super intendant Rodger Jacobs. Mr Jacobs can you tell us how you plan to enforce the increasing number of restrictions being placed on people, not just the vaccine status checks but the recent anti protesting laws the government voted through only last night?"

“Yes, the police officers under my command have the power to arrest and detain any person or persons breaching the restrictions. We have the right to force businesses to close if they are flaunting the laws.” The chief copper started speaking.

“What laws?” a shout came from Mark, next to me. The presenter immediately turned to mark. “Yes sir, what did you want to say.

“These are not laws, chief super intendant, as you well know and as Sarah just said, they are just statutes, acts and mandates, and the statutes, acts and mandates of this corrupt and treasonous government are only enforceable with the consent of the governed, that is the individual consent, not the collective consent of the men and women, and as a man here today I have removed my consent to be governed or to have government policies forced onto me. Your officers have no rights, power or authority over men and women unless a crime has been committed, and for there to be a crime, there has to be a victim, so going to the pub, shopping, working, opening your business or visiting a sick relative is not a crime. I will say it again, your jurisdiction is over the legal fiction not the man or woman unless a crime has been committed. If there is no victim there is no crime. Your officers take an oath to the King to uphold the laws of the land and not the rules of a corporation masquerading as government. So how do you propose to force these rules onto us when we are not committing crimes?" you could hear the passion on Marks voice as he spoke.

"That simply isn't true, when the government makes a law, we have the power to," The super intendant started to speak But Mark cut him off.

"The government is a corporation, registered on a company's website, and guess what, your company is on there to, currently trading under West Mainland police service ltd. You are currently the CEO and your corporation made profits of nearly six million pounds last year. This pretty much makes you a private security firm hired by another firm, currently trading as UK government plc. So, tell me again why I, as a man, have any business with you or your employees?" Mark fired into him. He had no answer.

"Where does your company's profit come from Mr. Jacobs? In fact, don't answer that. Your profit comes from unlawfully fining men and women. Tricking us into doing business with you. Giving out unlawful fines for breaking the rules made up by the corporation calling itself government. There was a law that was repealed by government that was written in the Bill of Rights that Sarah mentioned earlier. It stated, only a judge can fine you, in a court of law and that is after a trial by jury Mr. Jacobs. According to the rules made up by the government, you can fine us, headteachers can fine us, a machine at the side of the road can fine us, a van with a camera in it can fine us, and the list goes on and on. They are all unlawful fines. Most of these fines for victimless rule breaking are lining the pockets of private companies. You have no right to fine anybody." Mark finished and got a small cheer.

"I, Erm, I" Was the best answer the Chief super intendant could come up with.

"Well, who said crime doesn't pay? Mr. Williams, can we come back to you please. Will your business survive another set of rules being made up by the government." The presenter asked, deliberately changing the word laws for the word rules.

"Richard my business will not only survive, but it will thrive. When I leave here tonight, I will be contacting every one of my employees and asking them to come back to work tomorrow. I will no longer be obeying the rules of the two people sitting opposite me, and I will not be doing any business with Chief super intendant Jacobs or any of his employees. I apologize to my employees for going along with this nonsense and I hope they will forgive me." Mr. Williams replied with determination. A loud cheer came from every single member of the audience and even the technicians doing the broadcasting were clapping.

"If you disobey the laws I will personally come to your factory and arrest you myself Mr. Williams" the chief copper interjected.

"If you and your employees come to my factory you will be turned away, and to be honest with you I am pretty sure I have the right to defend myself and the people who work for me. Just because you stick a fancy uniform on and wave some silly piece of plastic warrant card about doesn't give you any power over me if I haven't hurt anyone. I have taken onboard what Sarah has said this evening. It didn't register with me until Sarah just said that if there is no victim then there is no crime, and I am certain that opening my business and providing employment so my employees can live is not a crime. Leave me alone and will leave you alone, all we are trying to do is live." Mr. Williams had put the copper in his place.

“As I just said Mr. Williams, you will obey the laws, or you will be arrested and put before magistrates.” The super intendant snapped back.

“Gentlemen please, let’s just calm down.” The host stepped in to stop any arguing. “Let’s get a question from the audience. The young man at the back there.” He pointed to the back of the hall where a young lad had his hand raised. The lad waited a few seconds for the microphone to reach him.

“I was recently raided by the police, and I was charged for possession of cannabis and growing cannabis Mr. Jacobs, I had six plants for my own use, this was seized, and I was cautioned for possession, and I am being prosecuted for cultivation. How can you justify this when there was no victim Mr. Jacobs?” the lad asked.

“Because young man, cannabis is a dangerous class B drug, and the law says we can prevent the use and supply of it. Now you can spout all this nonsense about victims and rules, but anyone caught growing, supplying or in possession of it will be prosecuted." The copper replied.

"Does that include everyone Mr. Jacobs?" the lad asked. A smile crept across my face as I already knew where he was going with this, and a worried look spread across Mrs. Fellows' face because she knew where he was going with this too.

"Yes, young man. Anybody pushing this dangerous drug should be punished." The superintendent replied.

"Well Mrs. Fellows husband and the husband of another MP have a facility about two hundred miles south of here that grows tons and tons of cannabis for export to the United States. In fact, the other politician is currently the governments spokesperson for drugs and recently said that "Cannabis is a dangerous drug and has no medicinal benefits whatsoever." But this doesn't stop her husband producing tons of it every year for sale as a medicine in America. can I ask how you can allow this to happen?" The young man smirked as he was speaking. The politician looked at the copper and the copper looked at the politician.

"We will have to look into this but I'm sure if any laws are being broken, we will prosecute those involved." Was the best answer the copper could come up with.

"It's all legal chief inspector, my husband has a license and special permission from the home office to grow and sell this drug for use in America. I can assure the public that none of this drug ever ends up on the streets over here." Mrs. Fellows retorted.

"So, what you're saying is that some of your friends in government have given your husband special permission to break the law. Don't you think the laws are there for us all, or are certain people exempt." The host stirred the pot with his comment. I raised my hand, but the host went back to the man who asked the question. "The young man who asked the question, would you like to add anything else."

"Yes, Richard I would. Where can I get some of this special permission from? I had the weed confiscated and was cautioned for a very small amount of this drug that you claim is dangerous. There are zero deaths from cannabis each year, it is helping millions of people worldwide with various illnesses and ailments, and recreationally, getting high is much like the effects of alcohol but without the violence and the liver damage. Can I also point out that your husband's company didn't pay a single penny in tax from growing weed last year and no doubt he won't this year either?" The young man finished talking and got a small round of applause. I raised my hand as there was more to say on this subject.

"Yes, Sir what would you like to add." The host gestured in my direction and the large microphone moved towards me.

"I would like to point out that it is us the people that give you permission to govern us. We can't give you something that we don't have, so if we don't have the right to do things like grow weed then we can't give you that right to give away. You have been caught out again cheating. Giving yourselves permission to break the rules because there are huge profits to be made." I paused to let her hang herself some more.

"My husband is allowed to conduct his business with America because its legal over there." Was the lame answer she gave.

"Your husband is growing and distributing a dangerous class B drug that has no medicinal benefits. Those are the words of one of your colleagues whose husband is in the weed business too. It doesn't matter that its legal where he is selling it but what does matter is that its illegal where he's growing it." I gave her more rope.

"It has medicinal benefits for people in America." She stopped speaking abruptly.

"Ha. So, what your saying is that human beings in America are getting benefits from using it but it's too dangerous for the British to use it because we are a different type of human being. Aren't we all biologically all the same Mrs. Fellows? Or could it be that you lot haven't quite worked out how to fleece us all for as much money as possible before you do a u turn and say, "Its ok peasants, we have decreed that you mere mortals have our special permission to do what we are doing, but you will have to give us lots of money if you want to do it." This got a loud cheer from the crowd. Mrs. Fellows had no reply for me.

"Can I also point out that if you are now giving licenses out to grow cannabis then all that young man has done is grow weed without a license, which would make it a civil matter, not a criminal matter, so Mr. Jacobs any criminal prosecution of this man should be stopped." I added.

"I assure you it is a criminal offence, and he will be punished." The copper barked back.

"Mr. Jacobs you seem to be playing by and making up your own rules here. What's good for the goose is good for the gander." I left it at that.

"Ladies and gentlemen, we seem to have gone off the subject of tonight's show. Can I ask Chief Super Intendant Jacobs about his forces recent handling of the peaceful rally held in the city on Saturday? There were reports of heavy-handed tactics from your officers, some were even filmed being violent towards people who were clearly not causing trouble. Can you justify the use of force against innocent people?" The presenter regained control of the questioning.

"My men were faced with a violent mob of several hundred people. They were spreading lies and disinformation and I deemed it appropriate to put a stop to it. My men are highly trained and used only the necessary force to prevent a breach of the peace." The copper lied through his teeth. Several hands went up in the crowd including mine and Marks, but the host went to a lady over to my right.

"The lady with the white blouse." The host gestured with his hand in the direction of the lady and the sound engineer did his thing with the microphone.

"You used violence to prevent peaceful people from breaching the peace. Men wielding batons, wearing crash helmets and carrying shields charged into the crowd who were just listening to people speak the truth Mr. Jacobs. You're not telling the whole truth though, are you? Your men got a little surprise didn't they Mr. Jacobs. For the benefit of the audience, I can confirm that sixty-five policy enforcement officers were arrested for crimes against the people. Including assault with deadly weapons, breaching the peace, affray and violent conduct. They were immediately outnumbered, which surprised them. They were arrested without any injuries, their numbers and warrant cards were taken, they were processed and are expected to appear in the common law court that we the people have convened to deal with this matter" the lady left the audience open mouthed.

"You have no right to arrest police officers Miss, and I will be talking to you after this show to find out what your involvement was." The copper squealed.

"Rodger Jacobs, I have no business with you or the corrupt corporation that you work for, but what will be happening is you will be arrested and tried under common law for giving the orders to attack people. Now you can claim you were just doing your job, but it didn't work at Nuremburg, and it won't work now. You are here to serve us, Mr. Jacobs. You took an oath to the King and so did your men. They did not take an oath to this corrupt and treasonous government. You swore to cause the peace to be kept. How is beating people with batons in any way keeping the peace?" The lady had venom in her voice and glared at the copper as she spoke.

"Can I just add that Nuremburg was another example of governments being reminded that the people are sovereign and have the final say over what is done with their bodies. Nothing at all can be done to a sovereign individual without their consent. This is mainly for you doctors and physicians out there, point number one of the Nuremberg codes is, the voluntary consent of the human subject is absolutely essential. The person involved should have a legal capacity to give consent and should be so situated as to be able to exercise freedom of choice without any element of force, fraud, deceit, duress or coercion. "Sarah added to reinforce the argument.

“I’ll tell you what you lot are, Your no better than terrorists. We will deal with anyone spreading disinformation just like terrorists.” The copper fired back, addressing nobody in particular.

“Mr. Jacobs the definition of terrorism is the unlawful use of violence and intimidation, especially against civilians, in the pursuit of political aims. Which is exactly what you and your men are doing when you attack innocent people to force the politicians will onto us. The truth was being spoken at the rally Mr. Jacobs and it didn’t fit the political narrative.” The lady in the audience calmly answered back.

“I heard some of what was spoken at the rally and its nonsense, something about the magna carta and not obeying laws. Utter rubbish.” He fired back at the lady.

“Mr. Jacobs article sixty-one of the magna carta was enacted on March the twenty third, two thousand and one. Article sixty-one is the security clause that once invoked should ensure us redress, but as usual it has been brushed under the carpet because it doesn't suit the narrative. Every man and woman should be standing in lawful rebellion against this corrupt government. We have a right to say, "no more" we have a right to protest, and we have a right to defend ourselves against you and your men. Choose your side, Mr. Jacobs, but choose wisely. The people have had enough. We can see through the lies; we can see through the deception. This is your wake-up call. We outnumber you and you men, thousands to one. We stand above you in honesty, decency and integrity. You work for us. We pay your wages and your gold-plated pensions, that goes for you politicians too. You are criminals." With that the young lady sat down. She got a round of applause from the audience, even some of the film crew joined in.

"I suppose you have something to add to that?" the copper barked at Sarah.

"No, the lady said exactly what I was about to say. Mr. Jacobs. Article sixty-one is not a myth. It's not fake or something to be ignored. This treasonous government should be brought to justice." Sarah replied calmly.

"Mr. Jacobs, would you be willing to investigate the allegations of treason." The host added.

"No, there is nothing to investigate. I won't waste any time on this nonsense." The copper replied.

"Can I add that my party has been looking into corruption within the current government and if we get into power at the next general election, we promise to release our findings." Mrs. Fellows seized the opportunity to promote her party.

"Mrs. Fellows your party is the left wing and Mr. Higgins party is the right wing but it's the same bird. You promise to look into corruption and release the findings "IF" you are elected and come into power. Like the gentleman in the audience said earlier you are elected to service not power and if there is any corruption, then we as your employers should know about it without being bribed." Mr. Williams added.

"Mr. Williams the government is not corrupt or treasonous. We recently investigated ourselves and found no wrongdoing whatsoever." Mr. Higgins joined back in.

I raised my hand along with nearly half of the audience. The host went to a gentleman to the front and left of me. The man who looked to be in his seventies cleared his throat then began to speak. "Do you think you did a thorough investigation Mr. Higgins? Do you not remember your business dealings with the convicted drug smuggler or how about one of your colleagues being involved in money laundering? What about the drugs business that the young man mentioned earlier? The expenses scandal. Giving contracts to family members, Mr. Higgins, what was the cost of those plastic aprons £5 each? No that wasn't enough for you was it, I mean why charge £5 when you can get the government to pay £10 per apron and even better, who was the company director of Medidress Mr. Higgins oh that's right, it was your wife wasn't it. I use past tense there

Mr. Higgins because she folded the company that she ran in her maiden name didn't she. How much tax did the company owe Mr. Higgins, I mean those aprons that normally cost fifty pence a unit to buy, soon add up when you start buying them from your own wife for £10 a time don't they? How much is enough Mr. Higgins? Haven't you got a big enough house? Haven't you got enough cars or is it the holidays that you like Mr. Higgins? My pension is £141 per week because I was stupid enough to work all my life. I have a small private pension that I put away for forty-two years and it doesn't even cover the cost of the unlawful council tax that I am coerced into paying every month. How much is your pension Mr. Higgins?" The man finished talking.

"My wife's business affairs are private, and I'm not willing to discuss my pension here. It's your responsibility to save for your old age sir. If you didn't put money away, then that's your own fault." The arrogant politician retorted.

“How are we supposed to save for old age when everything is taken from us when we are working. Seventy or eighty percent of my income in some way or another ended up back in the pockets of the government. You tax every single thing we do, it’s no more than a protection racket. As long as you get your percentage then you leave us alone, but it doesn’t stop at income tax does it, and if we don’t pay then you are willing to force us, coerce us and even jail us, but you don’t pay income tax do you? You are paid with tax money, you don’t produce, make, mend anything or help in any way to contribute to the coffers. Even when your wife earned around eight million pounds before your little business arrangement was discovered, she bumped the company owing the tax man a fortune but guess what, nothing will be done again will it?” the man was roasting the politician.

“I pay income tax like any other person sir, you are mistaken” The politician growled.

“It’s you who are mistaken sir. You are paid with tax money from the coffers. If we pay you a thousand pounds a week you should pay £200 tax, but guess what, the coffers just go down by £800 instead. The £200 never leaves the coffers. Then you don't even have the decency to pay the tax on the money you paid your wife for the plastic aprons." The man had run out of steam now and stopped talking. I raised my hand and caught the hosts' attention.

"Yes, sir what would you like to add." The host gestured in my direction. I waited for the microphone to be close enough to hear me.

"A contribution is a gift or payment to a common fund or collection; well, I no longer wish to contribute to a terrorist organization or pay criminals each week for lining their own pockets and the pockets of their friends." I cast the bait and waited to see which politician bit.

"Are you suggesting that the government is a terrorist organization? Are you mad sir?" It was good old Mr. Higgins who took the bait.

"I'm not suggesting anything Mr. Higgins. When I looked up the definition of contribution I also looked up the definition of terrorism and guess what terrorism is defined as, the unlawful use of violence and intimidation, especially against civilians, in the pursuit of political aims, then coupled with the law that says its unlawful to fund terrorism, I was wondering how we the people can lawfully contribute to your tax schemes when they are used to fund the murder of men, women and children in other countries for the pursuit of your political aims?" I stopped talking and waited for the politician to hang himself.

"We use the tax money how we see fit and if some of that money must be used for war then so be it. We are freeing the people in the other countries sir, not murdering them." The politician retorted.

"You are certainly liberating them Mr. Higgins. You liberate them of their oil, their gold and precious minerals, you steal their way of life and introduce your twisted version of freedom onto them. I live under your twisted version of freedom Mr. Higgins and at the moment it is costing me nearly every bit of energy that I create each week, you are stealing the energy that we create every day, you have no right to murder men, women and children to further your political agendas, and you will not do it with money or energy stolen from me. I no longer want anything to do with your wars or your rules, and I'm pretty sure from listening to the people here tonight that the majority of the people have had enough of you and the other criminals you work with." I stopped and awaited the politician's response. I glanced over at the chief copper and noticed he was hastily messaging on his phone which he was holding to the side of his leg so as not to draw attention to himself.

"The government has the right to," The politician started to talk but as the microphone hadn't been moved from near my face, I cut him off.

"The government is a fictitious entity Mr. Higgins. It is a creation of man therefore it is below man; it has no power over the men and women. The governments jurisdiction is over the fictional entities that it has created MR JOHN SMITH and MRS JANE

DOE. By trying to govern me you are saying you are above me and that is not true. I am man, nothing more, nothing less. You are man, nothing more, nothing less." I hadn't finished but it was the politicians turn to but in.

"Will you let me finish please. The government has the right to ensure the safety of the law-abiding citizens. We create new laws to ensure we can protect people from criminals and from enemies overseas." The politician replied unconvincingly.

"The only rights the government has are the rights people like you have given it, its men and women like you, hiding anonymously behind a word. You have currently been involved in lowering taxes for your millionaire friends, it wasn't the fictional thing that you hide behind that was doing it. You are involved in raising taxes for the working men and women. It's you the man, not the fictional entity you have created, and that appears to be blameless, that steals our wages. When men and women die in another country because you want the countries natural resources, it's you that is making that decision not the thing you hide behind. You and your co-conspirators are making the decisions that are affecting our lives on a daily basis. You will no longer be anonymous Edward Higgins; you will no longer keep secrets from your employer." I paused to take a breath or two.

"We have the right to keep secrets. We can't have every Tom, Dick and Harry knowing what's going on" The politician dug a deeper hole.

"And there it is folks. They rely on secrecy to do what they are doing. Mr. Higgins, I think it would be better if we had full disclosure from you and your colleagues from now on although I'm sure you will have created some rule or fake law that says you can remain anonymous. Put your name to the nonsense you are creating Mr. Higgins so we can hold you the man accountable for your actions." I was going to continue but I was cut short by the host.

"Ladies and Gentlemen, we have gone a little off subject again, it's clear that emotions are running high at the moment but let's get back on topic. Chief super intendant Jacobs can I ask what new powers you have been given to break up protest and demonstrations in relation to the vaccine mandates and movement restrictions being imposed onto the people."

"The movement restrictions are necessary for the protection of everybody; therefore, my officers have the right to stop any person and obtain their details. We have the right to break up illegal gatherings and fine any event organizers. We can use reasonable force when provoked, and we can use our weapons when we need to. These are laws written down in black and white, before you all start spouting your nonsense." The copper stared straight at me as he spoke.

It was clear that the sound engineer wanted to hear my response as he still hadn't moved the microphone. "Can I see proof of your right to use weapons against men and women who are concerned about their freedoms being taken. Can I see proof of your right as a man to harm another human being because some criminals don't like what is being said. The burden of proof is on the claimant, Mr. Jacobs, so prove you have the right to harm me, or I will certainly prove I have the right to defend myself and others from you. The men and women fighting for the few rights that we have left are not the enemy. The men and women standing up to the criminals masquerading as a lawful government are the people who can see what is happening.

The stench of corruption is hanging heavily in the air, Mr. Jacobs, but guess what, it's going to be ok because the politicians have made up another law that says we can no longer criticize them, we can no longer say no to them. Our overlords have granted us the right to protest quietly. We can walk down the road in a maximum group of three people, but woe betide us if we shout. Can you answer me this, Mr. Jacobs. Three weeks ago, there was a climate change demonstration in the city. There were large groups of people shouting, cheering, banging drums and waving banners and there was not a single arrest. No vaccine passports were checked, no identification was taken. The people were not harassed in any way. The police officers were even filmed joining in. My question is, do you only force the rules onto people who are not following the current political narrative like the men and women who stood up to you on Saturday, whose only crime was to stand peacefully listening to information before they were attacked?" I paused to let him answer.

"The people at Saturdays rally were violent thugs, and they were dealt with appropriately by my officers." The copper lied.

"The only violent thugs at the rally were your men Mr. Jacobs, but you are correct, they were dealt with appropriately. As the lady said earlier, a rally to spread the truth was held on Saturday in the city. Mr. Jacobs men attacked a nonviolent crowd and were immediately outnumbered, arrested and processed. The fake news showed the start of the rally then cut to old footage of another rally where the thugs were again beating innocent people." There were a few gasps from the audience. I caught a glimpse of yellow out of the corner of my eye. It was two policy enforcement officers. They moved quietly along the back of the room. I nudged Mark who just nodded to let me know he had seen them.

"I think we need to have a little chat with you after the show Sir" Super intendant Jacobs glared at me as he spoke.

"I have absolutely no business with you or the corporation you work for Roger Jacobs. You are a man, nothing more and nothing less. You need proof of claim over me and ultimately proof of authority, you have neither" It was my turn to glare at the copper now.

"Gentlemen, gentlemen please. Let's just take a step back here." The host interjected. "Mr. Higgins, can I ask about your comments recently. You said something about us all paying the money back that we received during the lock downs, you said the government were good enough to help everyone out, but it was just a loan. Can you elaborate on this."

"The money given to people and businesses will have to be paid back. We can't just go around giving money out and getting nothing back." There was a loud gasp from the audience. One of the film crew signaled the host that there were five minutes remaining, by holding up his outspread hand and mouthing the word five.

The microphone was still above my head. I glanced over and looked the sound engineer dead in the eye, and he just gave me a slight nod. "All you gave us was our own money back Mr. Higgins. It's the energy you have been stealing for years. The government takes out loans from the bankers and because there is no real money to pay the loans back with, you pledge our future earnings as surety for these loans, you have put the future earnings of millions of men and women up as a promise to the bankers. This makes us slaves, Mr. Higgins. You take out these loans and promise that us slaves will work even harder to pay your debts back.

You're not content with that though are you. You pay us with worthless slave tokens in the form of fiat money, these tokens can only be spent in the plantation shops and businesses, shops and businesses that must be registered to operate, and as we know, anything registered is given to the crown. You're not content that we work our lives away on the plantation, so you charge us some slave tokens each week for the privilege, you increase the amount of slave tokens on a regular basis, so we work even harder to get more slave tokens. You charge us to sleep on the plantation and eat on the plantation that our energy has built. When the slaves get out of line and start to stand up to you, you get other slaves to beat us down. If the petty thief steals from another slave you take no notice, but if a slave starts to steal from the masters, then he is heavily punished.

I don't want to be held as surety for your debts anymore, Mr. Higgins. I don't want to work my life away to pay your debts off. It's us that creates the energy necessary for all this to work, and we don't mind giving a little away to help the needy, but five or six days a week, for over fifty years, is a bit excessive. We don't want to pay for your invasion of other countries to enslave their populations. This country is bankrupt Mr. Higgins us slaves should have no debts because we are the solution to your problems, and you are the creator of ours." The audience sat in silence staring at the politicians, Mr. Higgins hung his head in shame.

I continued after a brief pause to let my words sink in "Mr. Jacobs," I addressed the copper again, "what is ironic is that you are sat on the stage with two criminals and because of your beliefs in their rules, you are more likely to arrest the decent hard-working Mr. Williams for allowing unvaccinated slaves to work at his business, and you would rather arrest Sarah for speaking the truth, instead of the two politicians. Answer me one more question, Mr. Jacobs. When they make up a new rule saying you must round up the slaves and put them in quarantine camps will you enforce the rule." I paused to let him answer but an angry look crossed his face.

"Officers, arrest that man, and that woman." He ordered, pointing at me, then at the young lady who spoke earlier. I spun around in my chair ready to stand up and fight but the two officers who had entered the building only moments earlier didn't budge an inch. I recognized the one copper as the young man who came to my door unarmed earlier in the week, but I couldn't remember his name.

"Can I ask what I am arresting them for sir?" The young copper responded to his superior.

"I don't know, anything, breach of the peace will do." The super intendant barked his order.

"I can't just arrest people for no reason sir, they need to have committed a crime. Where is the victim sir." The copper answered bravely defying the order.

“Damn well arrest them now or,” but that was as far as he got as the young copper cut in.

“Or what sir. Are you threatening me in front of all these witnesses? I think I would rather hear the answer to the question you were asked. So, if they decide to round up all the unvaccinated people based on some bullshit rule, or some undisclosed reason will you be expecting me and my colleagues to enforce their nonsense?” The young copper bravely defied Mr. Jacobs again.

“I will not answer to you. I am your superior, constable. Now arrest that man there, and that woman.” The older copper barked again pointing in turn to me then the young lady.

“You just addressed me as constable, sir. So, as a police constable who is standing on his oath of office, I will ensure the laws of the land are upheld and I will ensure the peace is kept, but unless this man or that woman has committed a crime then they have no business with me.” The young copper replied defiantly.

"Gentleman please. We are nearly finished here. Can we sort this out later. We are in the last moments of the show. Sir, would you have the final word please." The host gestured in my direction and the sound engineer moved the microphone into place above my head.

"It's clear by the actions of the crew here tonight that they want to hear the answers to the questions. The cameras have not stopped rolling, the sound man has not stopped doing his job. No doubt there are people behind the scenes that could have pulled the plug on tonight's broadcast but guess what they didn't, because they want the answers to, the people watching this broadcast want the truth for a change, the audience in here want the truth, the police officers are questioning your motives too. We employ you to sort out the day-to-day running of this country, we allow you to vote for your own pay rises. We have given you the opportunity to work hard and get everything sorted out but all you create is a mess. If I did my job as badly as you lot, I would be sacked, if I stole from my employer I would be out on my ear. If I tricked people, lied, manipulated, defrauded and murdered people I would be in jail, but you seem to think it's acceptable, it's just part of daily business for you and your friends.

We are fed up with your nonsense, I am hoping there will be a criminal investigation into your affairs because there are sixty-seven million people in this country that are getting fed up with watching every penny, they earn slipping from their fingers to go into this shitshow you have created. We will no longer pay your unlawful fines; we will no longer attend your mickey mouse courts and we want redress. Now I suggest when this show is over that you call whoever you need to call and arrange to be back in parliament tomorrow morning, bright and early, make up something about voting for your next pay rise and I'm sure you will all be there. Get it sorted out, it's your last chance. My voice is but one of millions, but it will be heard, I can't speak for everybody, but I speak for the majority when I say enough is enough. Thankyou." And with that I sat down.

"Thank you, sir, and thank you to our guests, our audience and you the viewers at home. I'm Richard Jones and this has been, well, interesting. Good night." The host wrapped up the show, and the audience including me gave a round of applause.

The lights came back on in the hall and we slowly stood up and started preparing to leave. Mark nudged me and as I looked up, I saw a rather angry looking Rodger Jacobs heading my way, pushing people out of his way. I dropped my right leg back and prepared to defend myself.

"Your fucking lot won't win. We will have the lot of you" the copper barked in my face.

"We have already won Mr. Jacobs. We are on the side of good." I spoke calmly but kept my arms at chest height ready to fend off any attack.

“Is everything ok here sir” the young copper stepped in between us and stared at the super intendant.

“Everything’s fine constable. Mr. Jacobs just came over to wish me well with our struggles.” I replied.

“I’ll be seeing you soon mate” the older copper barked poking me in the chest.

“That was assault sir. Do you want to press charges against this man.” The young copper said as he raised his hand to prevent Mr. Jacobs touching me again.

“No thankyou constable, he’s really not worth it.” I replied staring the older copper in the eyes.

Mr. Jacobs turned on his heels and walked off, not even looking back.

“My name is Stuart.” The young copper said as he extended his hand in my direction.

I shook Stuart firmly by the hand as I spoke. “Well, I don’t use names Stuart, as they are legal fictions, but I am commonly called

Dan. I'm a hard-working man who means no one any harm, but as you know I do stand up for myself and others. I hope you overstand why we have had to do things the way we did them. Did you investigate the information I gave you."

"Yes, I did, and it appears there's some work for us to do." He replied humbly.

"Arrest the criminals Stuart and you will have the full backing of the people. We are not the enemy. Question your orders and who and why they want certain things done. We shouldn't be living in fear of the people we pay to run things and we shouldn't be the victims of scams either. If you continue to uphold the laws of the land and not the laws of the sea, then you will be on the right track my friend." I extended my hand and as Stuart shook it Mark placed his hand on top as if to seal the deal.

Several people came over for a quick chat, or to pat us on the back. I went and found the young lady who was at the rally, who was not afraid to speak up. I introduced myself and Mark. We exchanged numbers the old-fashioned way with a borrowed pen and a scrap of paper. I shook the hand of the man who brought up the cannabis question and finally I found the host and thanked him for keeping the show going, he assured me they usually had several million viewers as the show was on at a prime time. I shook him warmly by the hand as we parted company. We got a thumbs up from some of the crew members and a pat on the back from the security lads as we exited the building.

The fresh air hit us as we left the building and me and Mark breathed a sigh of relief. "Fancy a pint Kidda?" Mark asked.

"Yes, mate I'm buying." I replied with a smile.

Afterword

Thank you, my friend, you have given life to me, the fictional character in this book, just like you give life to your legal fiction. You gave me a voice of your choosing. It was you that spoke the words that defeated the unlawful policy enforcement, and it was you that got angry or emotional at what you had created. The life I lived in your imagination for as long as it took you to read these words was hopefully thought provoking. You created hope with every word you spoke. You stood up and said enough is enough. You started to fight back and stand up for yourself. It felt good didn't it. I couldn't have fought back without you. I needed you to question the authority of the policy enforcement officers, and the politicians. I needed you to look at their rules and question them, and I needed you to take back your consent. Now do it for real my friend while there is still time. You are sovereign, you are the highest authority over you, it's you that has the power.

The end for me is the beginning for you.

Printed in Great Britain
by Amazon

61153884R00188